CARING FOR
HIS BABY

CARING FOR HIS BABY

BY

CAROLINE ANDERSON

MILLS & BOON™

Pure reading pleasure

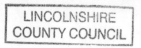
First published in Great Britain 2007
Large Print edition 2008
Harlequin Mills & Boon Limited,
Eton House, 18-24 Paradise Road,
Richmond, Surrey TW9 1SR

© Caroline Anderson 2007

ISBN: 978 0 263 20033 1

Set in Times Roman 16¾ on 20 pt.
16-0308-48232

Printed and bound in Great Britain
by Antony Rowe Ltd, Chippenham, Wiltshire

PROLOGUE

CRISIS in night. Please contact us ASAP.

Harry Kavenagh stared at the message handed to him by the hotel receptionist, and felt a cold chill run through him. No. Not now. He wasn't ready.

He'd never be ready—not for this.

Still staring at the words, he rammed the fingers of his other hand through his hair, rumpling the dusty, sweaty strands even further. So what now? He turned the paper over, looking for more information, but there was nothing.

'When did they call?' he asked.

'This morning, sir. Just after you went out.'

Fingers suddenly unsteady and his heart thudding in his throat, he called the number from his room. Five minutes later he was in a car on the way to the airport, his mind still reeling.

He couldn't believe it was actually happening. Stupid. He ought to be able to. It had been his idea, after all. They'd wanted to turn off the machine weeks ago, with his agreement, but he'd seen enough loss of life. Too much. So he'd begged them to reconsider—exhausted, perhaps a little drunk and stunned by what they'd told him, he'd haggled them into submission.

They'd kept their side of the bargain. And now he had to keep his.

He swallowed, staring out of the window, not seeing the bombed-out buildings, the shattered lives all around him. A shell exploded a few streets away, but he barely noticed. It all seemed suddenly terribly remote and curiously irrelevant, because in the space of the next few hours, his whole life would change for ever.

She was tiny.

So small, so fragile looking, her fingers so

fine they were almost transparent under the special light. She needed the light because she was yellow. Jaundiced, apparently. Quite common in slightly prem babies. Nothing to worry about.

But Harry worried about it. He worried about all of it. How on earth was he supposed to look after her? She was just a little dot of a thing, so dainty, no bigger than a doll. Small for dates, they'd said. No wonder, under the circumstances.

He didn't want to think about that, about how he'd failed her mother. How he'd brought her here to London to keep her safe and then failed her anyway.

'How are you doing?'

He looked up at the nurse and tried to smile. 'OK. She was screwing her face up a minute ago. I think she might have a nappy problem.'

'Want to change it?'

He felt his blood run cold. No. His hands were too big. He'd hurt her...

'She won't break, you know,' the nurse teased gently. 'You'll be fine. I'll help you.'

So he changed her nappy—extraordinarily complicated for something so ordinary—and by the end of the day and a few more goes he'd mastered it, even managing to grip those tiny little ankles between his fingers without snapping her legs when he lifted her up to swap the nappies over or wipe her unbe-lievably tiny bottom.

Such soft skin. Such astonishing perfection, all those little fingers and toes, the nails so small he could hardly see them. She was a little miracle, and he was awed beyond belief.

And terrified.

The nurse—Sue, her name was, according to her badge—brought him a bottle and helped him feed her again, and she brought it all up all over him. Panic threatened to choke him, but Sue just laughed and cleaned her up, lent him a fresh scrub top and handed her back.

'Make her slow down. She's feeding too

fast—tip the bottle up a bit more so she doesn't get so much air. And wind her in between.'

In between what? And wind her? How? He'd never winded a baby in his life, and he was damned if he knew where to start.

With that, or with any of it.

He felt faintly hysterical, but that was probably lack of sleep and shock. He stifled the urge to laugh, but then his eyes prickled and he felt the panic rise again.

What on earth had he done?

The old Chinese proverb rang hollow in his ears. *If you save a life, it belongs to you.*

He stared down at her, this tiny girl who apparently was his, her transparent fingers wrapped around his little finger with incredible strength, and the panic receded a little, replaced by wonder.

She was amazing. Beautiful. Scary as hell, but astonishing.

And his.

Officially registered this morning as his daughter, in the presence of the registrar of births, marriages and deaths just round the corner from the hospital.

He'd registered her mother's death at the same time, armed with more forms and certificates from the hospital, and then he'd gone back there and asked to see Carmen's body, so frail, so young, but finally at peace. And he'd told her about the baby, and promised her he'd do for the baby what he'd failed to do for her—to keep her safe. So now, in every way that mattered, she was his.

'Get out of that, Kavenagh,' he murmured, but strangely he didn't want to. He couldn't imagine walking away from her. Just the thought of abandoning her to fate made him feel so fiercely protective it scared him.

Together with everything else today.

God, he was knackered. Maybe if he just propped her up on his chest and leant back…

'Harry?'

He opened his eyes a crack, blinking at the light, and Sue's face came into focus. 'Why don't you go and have a lie-down? There's a room here for parents—nothing flashy, just a few beds and a separate area with a TV and little kitchen, but you could sleep for a while.'

Sleep. Oh, yes. Please. He had to get some sleep. It had been weeks since he'd slept properly, with the constant shelling and rocket fire going on all night, but this had tired him more than any of that.

He nodded, realising that the baby was back in her crib under the light and that everything was being taken care of.

'Will she be all right?' he asked, as if his presence actually made a blind bit of difference, but the nurse just smiled and nodded.

'Sure. I'll look after her for you, I'm on till nine, and I'll hand her over to the night staff before I go. Come on, I'll show you the parents' room.'

A bed. Crisp white sheets, a slightly crackly pillow and almost instant oblivion...

'You'll be OK.'

He stared down at Sue, wishing he could

believe her. She'd spent the last few days telling him he could cope, showing him not just how to change nappies and hold feeding bottles, but bath and dress and simply cuddle his tiny daughter, and he'd begun to believe that maybe—just maybe—he'd manage. Till now.

She was so small, his little doll, but she was tough, like her mother—fierce and determined, and for something so tiny she had a blood-curling scream. He'd become almost confident, in the safe environment of the special care baby unit, surrounded by the bleeps and clicks of the equipment, the hurried footsteps, the laughter and the tears. But now…

'We're always here if you have a problem. You can ring at any time. You will cope, Harry,' Sue said again, as if by repeating it she could make it true, and stretching up on tiptoe, she kissed his cheek and went back inside, leaving him on the outside of the doors, stranded.

What was he supposed to do now? Where could he go? His flat? It was nothing more than a crash pad, really, and it didn't feel like his any longer, but stupidly until now he hadn't even thought about where he'd take the baby. Just not there. It didn't seem right. But where?

He looked down at his tiny girl in the shockingly expensive baby carrier he'd bought that morning, and his heart squeezed. She was staring up at him intently, her almost black eyes fixed on his face, and he found himself suddenly calmer.

He knew what to do, and it was more than time he did it. He should have done it years ago.

'Come on, my little Kizzy,' he murmured softly. 'We're going home.'

CHAPTER ONE

SOMEONE was moving in.

It had been weeks since the last tenants had left, but there was a car on the drive and the lights were on.

Emily craned her neck and tried to catch a glimpse of the people, but she couldn't see through the trees. Not clearly enough, anyway. The branches kept drifting softly in the light breeze and blocking her view, and every time she shifted, so did the leaves.

And she was turning into a curtain twitcher, for heaven's sake!

She snapped the curtain shut and turned her back on the window, tucking up Freddie and smiling down at him. Gorgeous. He was just gorgeous, and she wanted to scoop him up and snuggle him.

Except he'd wake in a foul mood and the sweet little cherub would turn into a howling, raging tyrant. The terrible twos were well named, and he wasn't even there yet, not for five months!

She grinned and tiptoed out, blowing him a kiss and pulling the door to, just a little, before checking on his big sister. Beth was lying on her back, one foot stuck out the side, her tousled dark hair wisping across her face.

Emily eased the strand away from her eyes and feathered a kiss over her brow, then left her to sleep. There was a film on television starting in a few minutes that she'd been meaning to watch. If she could get the washing-up stacked in the dishwasher, she might even get to see it.

Or not.

She hadn't even stepped off the last stair before she saw a shadow fall across the front door and a hand lift to tap lightly on the glass.

Her new neighbours?

She sighed inwardly and reached for the latch. She'd have to be polite. It wasn't in her to be anything else, but just for tonight it would have been nice to curl up in front of the television and be utterly self-indulgent. She'd even bought a tub of Belgian chocolate ice cream...

'Em?'

'Harry?'

Her hand flew to her mouth, stifling the gasp, and then her eyes dropped, dragging away from his to focus on...

A baby?

She blinked and looked again. Yes, definitely a baby. A tiny baby—very tiny, hardly old enough to be born, held securely against the broad chest she'd laid her head against so many times all those years ago.

'Oh, Harry!' She reached out and drew him in, going up on tiptoe to kiss his cheek and somehow resisting the urge to howl, because if there was a baby, then there was a woman, and if there was a woman...

She let him go before she did something silly. 'Gosh, it's been so long—how are you?' she asked, her voice not quite her own, her eyes scanning his face eagerly.

'Oh—you know.'

No, she didn't, despite seeing him on the television almost on a daily basis. She didn't have the slightest idea, but his mouth was twisting in a parody of a smile and he looked exhausted.

Actually, he looked a great deal more than exhausted. He looked fantastic. Tall, bronzed, his striking pale blue eyes crinkled at the corners from screwing them up in the sun in all the godforsaken trouble spots he spent his life in. He needed a shave, and his hair was overdue for a cut, the dark strands a little wild. Her fingers itched to touch them, to feel if they were still as soft as she remembered, but she couldn't. She didn't have the right. Apparently, while she hadn't been looking, he'd given that to some other woman.

He turned a fraction, so his head was blocking

out the light and she could no longer see his eyes, so she glanced down and her heart jerked against her chest. The tiny babe was all but lost inside the big, square hands that cradled it so protectively, the little head with wild black hair sticking out from under the edges of the minuscule hat cupped securely by long, strong fingers.

Such a powerful image. Advertising had recognised the power of it decades ago, but here it was now, standing in her hallway, and she felt her knees weaken.

Her resolve was turning to mush, as well.

'You're back,' she said eventually, when she could get her brain to work. 'I saw the lights on. I didn't think it would be you.' Not after all these years. Not after last time… 'Are you alone?'

'Yes. Just me and the baby.'

Just? *Just?* She nearly laughed out loud. There was nothing *just* about a baby, most especially not one that tiny. She wondered how long it would be before his wife joined them and rescued him. Later tonight? Tomorrow?

Although she hadn't heard that he was married, but then he hadn't stayed in touch with her or her brother Dan, and she didn't keep her ear that close to the ground.

Liar! her conscience shrieked. *Weekly checks on the Internet, avid scanning of the news, hanging on every word of his news reports...*

'So where's the baby's mother? Does she trust you?' she asked, just because she couldn't stand the suspense another minute.

His smile twisted, and there was a little flicker of what could have been panic, but his eyes were sombre and there was something in them she just couldn't read. 'No mother,' he said expressionlessly. 'It's just us—me and the baby.'

Hope leapt in her chest, and she squashed it ruthlessly. Quite apart from the fact that there was a story here he wasn't telling her, another go-round with Harry Kavenagh was absolutely the last thing she needed for her peace of mind, but his reply answered why he was here, anyway, and there was no way she was getting suckered into that one! He could cope with the baby on his own, thank you very much!

She pulled back, both physically and emotionally, trying to distance herself from him so she didn't get drawn in, but then the baby started to fuss, and a flicker of what was definitely panic ran over his face, and she had to steel herself against him.

'So—what can I do for you?' she asked, trying not to sound too brisk but giving him very little encouragement at the same time.

He looked a little taken aback—perhaps she'd been too brisk after all—but his shoulders lifted and he smiled a little tiredly. 'Nothing. I'm staying here for a bit, so I just came to see who was here, to introduce myself—say hello to your parents if they were still here. I wasn't sure…'

Was it a question? She answered it anyway, her mind still stalled on his words. *I'm staying here for a bit…*

'They're in Portugal. They live there part of

the year. Mum was homesick, and my grand-mother's not very well.'

'So you're house-sitting for them?'

'No. I live here,' she told him. And then wished she'd said 'we' and not 'I', so he didn't feel she was single and available. Because although she might be single again, she was very far from being available to Harry Kavenagh.

Ever again.

The baby's fussing got louder, and he jiggled her a bit, but he wasn't doing it right and she looked tense and insecure. Emily's hands itched to take the little mite and cradle her securely against her breast, but that was ridiculous. She had to get rid of him before her stupid, stupid hands reached out.

She edged towards the door. 'Sounds hungry. You'd better go and feed her—her?' she added, not sure if the baby was a girl, but he nodded.

'Yes.'

Yes, what? Yes, she's a girl, or, yes, he'd better feed her/him/it? She opened the door anyway, and smiled without quite meeting his eyes. 'I hope you settle in OK. Give me a call if you need anything.'

He nodded again, and with a flicker of a smile he went out into the night and she closed the door.

Damn. Guilt was a dreadful thing.

She walked resolutely down the hall, got the ice cream out of the freezer, contemplated a bowl and thought better of it, picked up a spoon and the tub and went into the sitting room, put on the television and settled down cross-legged on the sofa to watch her film.

Except, of course, it had started and she'd missed the point, and anyway her mind kept straying to Harry and the baby, so tiny in his hands, and guilt tortured her.

Guilt and a million questions.

What was he doing on his own with a baby? Was she his? Or a tiny orphan, perhaps, rescued from the rubble of a bombed out building…

And now she was being completely ridiculous. The baby was days old, no more, and the paperwork to get a baby out of a war-torn country would be monumental, surely? There was always the most almighty fuss if a celebrity tried to adopt a baby, and she was pretty sure he counted as a celebrity.

Unless he'd kidnapped her?

No. He had the slightly desperate air of a man who'd had a baby dumped on him—one of his girlfriends, perhaps, sick of his nonsense and fed up with trying to compete with the more exciting world he inhabited? Maybe she'd thought he needed a dose of reality?

Or perhaps she was dead, had died in childbirth…

'Oh, for goodness' sake!'

She put the ice cream back in the freezer, hardly touched, and stood at the kitchen window, staring out at the house next door.

She could hear the baby screaming, and the mother in her was heading down the hall and out of the door, a cuddle at the ready. Fortunately the pragmatist in her stayed rooted to the spot, wishing she had defective hearing and wasn't so horribly tuned in to the sound of a crying child.

She made herself a drink, went back to the sitting room and had another try at the television. Maybe another programme, something less dependent on her not having missed a huge chunk. She flicked though the channels.

A cookery programme, yet another make-over show, a soap she'd never watched and a documentary on one of the many messy wars that seemed to be going on all over the world.

Which took her straight back to Harry Kavenagh and the tiny crying baby next door…

'Hush, little one,' he pleaded, jostling her gently. 'Have a drink, sweetheart, you must be hungry. Is it too cold? Too hot?'

Hell, how was he supposed to know? He liked his coffee scalding hot and his beer ice-cold. Somewhere in between was just alien to him.

He stared in desperation at the house next door, the lights just visible through the screen of trees.

No. He couldn't go round there. She'd hardly greeted him with open arms, after all.

'Well, what the hell did you expect?' he muttered, swapping the baby to his other arm and trying a different angle with the bottle. 'You drop out of her life for years and then stroll back in with a baby in your arms—she probably thought you were going to dump the baby on her!'

He tightened his grip on his precious burden and the crying changed in pitch. Instantly he slackened his grip, shifted her to his shoulder and rubbed her back, walking helplessly up and down, up and down, staring at Emily's house as he passed the window.

The lights were out now, only the lovely stained-glass window on the stairs illuminated by the landing light. Strange. He didn't remember her being afraid of the dark. Maybe it was because she was alone in the house...

'Stop thinking about her,' he growled softly, and the baby started to fuss again. 'Shh,' he murmured, rubbing her back again and going into the bathroom. 'How about a nice warm bath?'

Except she pooed in it, and he had to change the water in the basin one-handed without dropping her, and then it was too hot and he had to put more cold in, and then it was too full, and by the time he got her back in it she was screaming in earnest again and he gave up.

He could feel his eyes prickling with despair and inadequacy. Damn. He wasn't used to feeling inadequate. 'Oh, Gran, where are you?' he sighed a little unsteadily. 'You'd know what to do—you always knew what to do about everything.'

He dried the baby, dressed her in fresh clothes and tried to put her in the baby-carrier, but she wasn't having any. The only way she'd settle at all was if he held her against his heart and walked with her, so he did exactly that.

He pulled his soft fleecy car rug round his shoulders, wrapped it across her and went out into the mild summer night. He walked to the cliff top and then down through the quiet residential roads to the prom, strolling along next to the beach and listening to the sound of the sea while the baby slept peacefully against his heart, and then when he could walk no more and his eyes were burning with exhaustion and he just wanted to lie down and cry, he took her home and sat down in the awful chair that the tenants had left and fell asleep.

Not for long.

Not nearly long enough. The baby woke, slowly at first, tiny whimpers turning gradually to a proper cry and then ultimately a full-blown blood-curdling yell by the time he'd found her bottle in the fridge and warmed it and tested it and cooled it down again by running it under the tap because of course he'd overheated it, and by the time he could give it to her she'd worked herself up to such a frenzy she wouldn't take it.

He stared down at her in desperation, his eyes filling. 'Oh, Kizzy, please, just take it,' he begged, and finally she did, hiccupping and sobbing so she took in air and then started to scream and pull her legs up, and he thought, What made me think I could do this? I must have been mad. No wonder women get postnatal depression.

He wondered if it was possible for men to get it. Clumsy, inadequately prepared fathers who'd never been meant to be mothers to their children—men whose wives had died in a bomb blast or an earthquake and left them unexpectedly holding the baby. Or men widowed when their wives died in childbirth. Or even men who'd taken the decision to be the house-husband and main carer of the children. How did they cope?

How did anyone cope?

He changed her, then changed her again when she was sick down her front, then gave her another little try with the bottle and finally put her down in the carrier, shut the door and went upstairs to the bedroom he'd used as a child, leaving her screaming.

He had to get some sleep if he was going to be any good to her.

But the only furniture in the room was a bare, stained mattress, and he couldn't bring himself to lie on it even if he could ignore the baby's cries for long enough to get to sleep.

He looked around him critically, taking in the state of the place properly for the first time, and realised that if he was going to live in it, it was going to need a team of decorators to come in and blitz it, new carpets and furniture through-out and probably a new kitchen.

And in the meantime he'd be living there with the baby?

He must have been insane.

He should have let the doctors throw the switch all those weeks ago instead of interfering.

Acid burned his stomach and he shook his head. No.

Whatever came next, what he'd done so far had been exactly the right thing. The only thing. And it would get easier. It had to. He'd learn to cope. And right now he was going back down-stairs, and he'd lift her out of the carrier and lie down on the grubby chair and cuddle her on his chest until they both went to sleep. The rest he could deal with tomorrow…

'I'm going to get you!'

Emily ran after her giggling son, chasing him down the garden and scooping him up, and straightened to find Harry standing on the other side of the fence staring at her and Freddie in astonishment.

'Um—hi,' he said. She smiled back and said, 'Hi, yourself. How's the baby?'

Freddie looked at him with the baby on his shoulder, gave his lovely beaming smile and said, 'Baby!' in his sing-song little voice and clapped his chubby hands in delight.

Now she'd had time to register it, Emily was too busy searching Harry's exhausted face to worry about the baby. There were deep black smudges under his eyes, and his jaw was shadowed with stubble. She ached to hold him, to stroke that stubbled chin and soothe the tired eyes with gentle fingers—'Are you OK?' she asked, trying to stick to the plot, and his eyes creased with weary humour.

'I'm not sure. I'm so tired I can't see straight at the moment. We had a bit of a problem in the night.'

'I heard,' she said, feeling guiltier still for her less-than-enthusiastic welcome the evening before. 'Um—look, why don't you come round and have a coffee? We're not doing anything, are we, Freddie? And we've got an hour before we have to pick up Beth.'

'Beth?' he said.

'My daughter.'

She wondered if he'd notice the use of 'my' and not 'our'. Maybe. Not that it mattered. If he was going to be living next to her for longer than ten minutes, he'd work out that she was alone. Anyway, she didn't think he was worrying about that at the moment. He was busy looking slightly stunned, and she wondered if she'd looked like that last night when she'd seen *his* baby for the first time.

Probably. She'd been shocked, because the last time they'd met, they'd both been single and free, and now, clearly, he wasn't. And as for her—well, she was single again, but far from free, and maybe it was just as much of a shock to him to know she was a parent as it had been to her to realise he was.

Because, of course, if she knew nothing about his private life for the last umpteen years, it was even more likely that he knew nothing about hers.

Or the lack of it.

He gave her a cautious smile. 'Coffee would be good. Thanks.'

Coffee? She collected herself and tried for an answering smile. 'Great. Come through the fence—the gate's still here.'

She opened it, struggling a little because the path was a bit mossy there and the gate stuck, and he grabbed it and lifted it slightly and shifted it, creaking, out of the way.

'The creaking gate,' he said, and added, with that cheeky grin that unravelled her insides, 'It always did that. I used to know just how far to open it before it would rat on me.'

And she felt the colour run up her cheeks, because she remembered, too—remembered how he'd sneak through the gate and meet her at the end of the garden in the summerhouse, late at night after everyone was asleep, and they'd cuddle and kiss until he'd drag himself away, sending her back to bed aching for something she hadn't really understood but had longed for anyway.

'We were kids,' she said, unable to meet his eyes, and he laughed softly.

'Were we? Didn't always feel like it. And the last time—'

He broke off, and she took advantage of his silence to walk away from the incriminating gate and back up the garden to the house, Freddie on her hip swivelling wildly round and giggling and shrieking, 'Baby!' all excitedly.

She really didn't want to think about the last

time! It should never have happened, and there was no way it was happening again.

She scooped up the runner beans from the step, shoved open the back door with her hip and went in, smiling at him over Freddie's head.

'Welcome back,' she said, without really meaning to, but she was glad she had because the weariness in his eyes was suddenly replaced by something rather lovely that reminded her of their childhood, of the many times she'd led him in through her parents' back door and into the welcome of their kitchen.

'Thanks.' He reached out and ruffled Freddie's bright blond curls. 'I didn't know you had kids.'

There was something in his voice—regret? She shot him a quick look, filed that one for future analysis and put the kettle on. 'Yup. Beth's three, nearly four, and Freddie's nineteen months. Real or instant?'

'Have you got tea? I daren't have too much caffeine. I had so little sleep last night I want to be able to grab every second of it that's offered!'

She laughed and reached for the teapot, lifting it down from the cupboard and putting Freddie on the floor. 'Darling, go and find your cup,' she instructed, and he trundled off, humming happily to himself.

'He's cute.'

'He is. He can be a complete monster, if it suits him, but most of the time he's gorgeous.'

Harry gave a strangled laugh. 'I wish I could say the same for this one, eh, Mini-Dot?'

'Mini-Dot?' she said, spluttering with laughter, and he chuckled.

'Well, she's so tiny. It's not her real name. Her real name's Carmen Grace—Kizzy for short.'

'Oh, that's pretty. Unusual.'

'Grace is for my grandmother.'

'And Carmen?'

His face went still. 'For her mother,' he said softly, and there was an edge to his voice that hinted at something she couldn't even begin to guess at. Maybe he would tell her later. She hoped so, because she didn't feel she could ask. Not now.

She would have done, years ago, but they'd spent every waking minute together in those halcyon days of their youth and there had been nothing they hadn't shared.

But now—now she didn't know him at all, and she didn't know how much he was going to give her, and how much she wanted to give back.

So she said nothing, just made them tea and found a few chocolate biscuits and put them on a plate. Then Freddie came back with his cup trailing a dribble of orange juice behind him, and she refilled it and mopped up the floor and hugged him, just because he was so sweetly oblivious and she loved him so much it hurt.

He giggled and squirmed out of her arms and ran out into the garden, and they followed him, she with the tray, Harry with the baby—Mini-Dot, for goodness' sake!—and she led him to the swinging seat under the apple tree.

'Is this the same one?' he asked in wonder, but she laughed and shook her head.

'No, it fell to bits. Dad bought a new one a few

years ago, so you don't have to sit down so carefully any more.'

He chuckled and eased himself down onto the seat, leaning back and resting his head against the high back and closing his eyes. 'Oh, bliss. This is gorgeous.'

'Bit of a change from your usual life,' she said without meaning to, and he cocked an eye open and gave a rusty little laugh.

'You could say that.' For a moment he was silent, then he sighed and opened his other eye and turned his head towards her. 'It takes a bit of getting used to—the quiet, the birdsong, the normal everyday sounds of people going about their daily lives. Crazy things that you wouldn't think about, like the sound of a lawnmower—when I can hear it over the baby, that is,' he added, his mouth kicking up in a rueful grin.

She answered him with a smile, then felt her curiosity rise. No. She wouldn't go there…

'What happened, Harry?' she asked softly, despite her best intentions.

His smile faded, and for a moment she didn't think he was going to answer, but then he started to speak, his voice soft and a little roughened by emotion. 'I found her—Carmen—sitting by the side of the road, begging. Every day I walked past her on my way from the hotel and gave her money. Then after four days she wasn't there. The next time I saw her, she'd been beaten up. Her mouth was split, one eye was swollen shut and the other one was dull with pain and despair. She wasn't expecting anything—a few coins, perhaps, nothing more—but I took her to a café and bought her breakfast, and talked to her. And it was only then that I realised she was pregnant.'

Emily clicked her tongue in sympathy. 'Poor girl.'

He nodded. 'She'd been raped, she told me. She didn't know the father of her child, it could have been any one of several men—soldiers. She'd didn't know which side they were on. It didn't really matter. She was a gypsy. They aren't highly regarded in Eastern European countries—

liars, thieves, lazy—you name it. And two nights before she'd been raped and beaten again. But she was just a girl, Emily, and she was terrified, and she'd lost her entire family.'

'So you took her under your wing,' she said, knowing that he would have done so, because he'd always been like that.

He gave a tiny hollow laugh. 'In a manner of speaking. I moved her into my hotel room, fed her, got a doctor for her, and while I was in the shower she stole my wallet and ran away. So I tracked her down and asked her why. Eventually she told me she was waiting for me to rape her.'

Emily asked again. 'So what did you do?'

'I married her,' he said quietly. 'To keep her safe. Ironic, really. I brought her home to London and installed her in my flat. I gave her an allowance, paid all the bills and saw her whenever I could. And gradually she learnt to trust me, but she was lonely. Then she started going out and meeting up with people from her country and she was much happier. She was learning English, too, at evening classes, and starting to make friends.'

He fell silent, and she waited, watching him, knowing he would carry on when he'd found the words.

'She was mugged. She was seven and a half months pregnant and someone mugged her on the way home from college one night. She ran away and crossed the road without looking and was hit by a car. She was taken to hospital, but she had a brain injury, and by the time they got hold of me she was on life support and they were doing brain-stem tests. So much for keeping her safe.'

The horror of it was sickening, and she put her hand over her mouth to hold back the cry. 'Oh, Harry, I'm so sorry,' she whispered.

'Yeah.' He swallowed. 'They didn't know whether to switch off the machine. They'd scanned the baby and it was fine, but they didn't know how I'd feel. I'd just flown in from an earthquake, I hadn't slept in days and I was exhausted. I didn't know what to say. I just knew I couldn't give up on the baby—not after everything we'd been through. She hadn't done anything wrong. She hadn't asked for this, and I've seen so many children die, Em, and not been able to do anything about it. And here was one I could do something about. I couldn't let her go. So I asked them to keep Carmen alive, long enough to give the baby a chance. And last week she ran out of time. Her organs started to fail, and they delivered the baby and turned off the machine. I got there just too late to say goodbye.'

He stared down at the baby on his lap, her mouth slack in sleep, her lashes black crescents against her olive cheeks, and Emily's vision blurred. She felt the hot splash of tears on her hands, and brushed them away.

'Harry, I'm so sorry,' she said again, and he looked up, his eyes haunted, and then looked down again at the precious bundle in his arms.

'Don't be. Not for me. I know it's hell at the moment and I feel such a muppet—I'm not used to being so phenomenally incompetent and out of my depth, but it will get better. I'll learn, and she's amazing. So lovely. So much perfection out of so much tragedy and despair. And I'm all she's got.'

Emily wanted to cry. Wanted to go into a corner somewhere and howl her eyes out for him, and for the baby's poor young mother, and for little Carmen Grace, orphaned almost before her birth.

'So that's us,' he said, his voice artificially bright. 'What about you?'

'Me?' she said, her eyes still misting. 'I'm, ah—I'm fine. I'm a garden designer—fitting it in around the children, which can be tricky, but I manage more or less. Get through a lot of midnight oil, but I don't have to pay for my accommodation at the moment.'

Although if her parents did sell their house, as they were considering doing, that would all change, of course.

'And their father?'

She gave a tiny grunt of laughter. 'Not around.

He didn't want me to keep Beth. Freddie was the last straw.'

Harry frowned. 'So what did he do?'

'He walked—well, ran, actually. I haven't seen lightning move so fast. I was four months pregnant.'

'So he's been gone—what?'

'Two years.'

Two difficult, frightening years that she would have struggled to get through without the help of her parents and her friends, but they'd all been wonderful and life now was better than it had ever been.

'I'm sorry.'

She smiled. 'Don't be. Things are good. Hang in there, Harry. It really does get better.'

He looked down at the baby and gave a twisted little smile. 'I hope so,' he said wryly. 'It needs to.'

'It will,' she promised, and just hoped that she was right...

CHAPTER TWO

FREDDIE'S CUP landed in her lap, dribbling orange on her, and she absently righted it and brushed away the drips.

Finally she looked back at him. 'So—aren't the legal ramifications vast? Nationality and so on?'

He shrugged. 'Apparently not. I was Carmen's husband, I'm down on the baby's birth certificate as her father. That makes her British.'

'But you're not. Her father, I mean. Couldn't that land you in trouble, if they ever found out?'

'How? Are you going to tell them? Because I'm not. I know it'll be hell, but I won't be the first father to bring up a child alone, and I doubt I'll be the last. And if not me, then who? The legalities are the least of my worries. I owe her this. It's the least I can do.'

The least he could do? Devoting his life to her? He was either even more amazing than she'd remembered, or utterly deluded.

Probably both. Rash and foolhardy, his grandfather used to say affectionately. But kind. Endlessly kind. He reached for his cup, the baby held against his shoulder by one large, firm hand, but her head lolled a little and his grip tightened and she started to cry again.

'Let me—just while you drink your tea,' she said, and reaching out, she lifted the tiny little girl into her arms.

'Oh—she's so small! I'd forgotten! They grow so quickly—not that Freddie was ever this small. Beth was dainty, but even she—'

She broke off, the baby's fussing growing louder, and she walked down the garden a few steps, turning the baby against her breast instinctively.

And with the same instinct, little Carmen

Grace nuzzled her, then cried again. Oh, poor lamb. She needed her mother!

'She's hungry,' she said, her voice uneven, and he got up and reached for her, but Emily shook her head, curiously reluctant to let the baby go.

'Bring the bottle. I'll hold her while you get it, it's all right.'

He hesitated for a second, then went, squeezing through the gate and returning a few moments later with a bottle. 'I don't know if it's the right temperature,' he said, handing it over, and Emily tested it on the inside of her wrist and frowned.

'It's too cold. I'll go and warm it. Keep an eye on Freddie for me.'

She went into the kitchen, gave the bottle a few seconds in the microwave, shook it vigorously and tested it again, then slipped the teat into the baby's mouth, silencing her cries instantly.

Good.

She went back down the garden and found Harry on his knees with Freddie, playing in the sandpit. As she walked down the garden he sat back on his heels and looked up at her with a relieved smile.

'Sounds peaceful.'

She laughed and settled herself on the bench, watching them and trying not to let her stupid thoughts run away with her.

'Did you love her?' she asked, then wanted to bite her tongue off, but he just sat back again and stared at her as if she was crazy.

'She was a child, Em. I married her for her own protection. Yes, I grew to love her, but not in the way you mean. It was just a legal formality, nothing more. I never touched her.'

She felt a knot of something letting go inside her, but she didn't want to think about the significance of that. She turned her attention back to the tiny scrap in her arms. The bottle was almost empty, the tiny amount she'd drunk surely not enough to keep her alive, but she was so small, her stomach must be the size of a walnut. Smaller.

She lifted her against her shoulder and rubbed her back, waiting for the burp and watching Harry as he piled sand into the bucket with Freddie and helped him turn it out.

'Mummy, castle!' Freddie shrieked, and the baby bobbed her head against Emily's shoulder, her whole body stiffening in shock. She soothed her with a stroking hand, rocking her and smiling at Freddie.

'I can see,' she said softly.

'How about a moat?'

'Wasa moat?' he asked, and Harry chuckled.

'It's like a big ditch full of water that goes all round the outside—here, like this,' he said, scraping out a hollow ring around the slightly wonky castle.

'You made one on the beach with Dickon and Maya last week,' Emily pointed out, and Freddie nodded and scrambled to his feet.

'Mummy, water!' he demanded, running to her with his cup, but Harry got up and grinned and ruffled his hair.

'Let her sit there for a minute. We'll get the

water. Come with me and show me where the tap is,' he said, and held out his hand.

Freddie, normally the last person to allow such a familiarity, slid his hand trustingly into Harry's and trotted happily beside him, chattering all the way to the kitchen.

Emily glanced down at the baby, sleeping again, her tiny face snuggled into the crook of her neck so that she could feel the soft skin, the warm huff of her breath, the damp little mouth, and the ache in her chest grew until she had to swallow hard to shift it.

'Poor baby,' she crooned, cradling her head with a protective hand. 'Don't worry, darling. We'll look after you.'

She didn't even think about the words. They came straight from her heart, bypassing her common sense, and as she rocked the baby in her arms, she felt a sense of rightness that should have rung alarm bells, but the bells were switched off, and the warning went unheeded.

* * *

Freddie was delicious.

Bright and bubbly, his fair hair sticking up on one side as if he'd slept on it. It was soft and unruly, much like Harry's own, and it felt just right under his hand.

''Nough?' Freddie asked, and Harry nodded, looking at the jug he'd found.

'I think it's enough.'

But, of course, it sank straight into the sand, and Freddie's excitement turned to disappointment.

'Mummy!' he wailed, running to her and throwing himself at her knees, and Harry felt racked with guilt because he'd suggested it and it had failed and now the boy was upset. Damn. Could he do nothing right?

Em looked up at him with an apologetic smile. 'There's a cake ring in the drawer under the oven,' she told him. 'It should just about fit over the castle. You could use that and fill it with water.'

So they went back up to the kitchen, and

found the cake ring, and with a bit of adjustment they fitted it over the sandcastle and filled it with water, and even found a stick to make a drawbridge and floated a leaf in it as a boat.

And the look on Freddie's face was priceless. 'Boat!' he said, and ran to his mother yet again, his eyes alight. 'Mummy, boat! 'Ook!'

Emily looked, admired it dutifully and threw Harry a smile over Freddie's head, then stood up. 'I have to get Beth,' she said, 'and I think this little one needs her daddy's attention.'

There was a spreading stain below her nappy, and Harry's heart sank. He wasn't sure if there was a washing machine in the house, and she'd only got a few clothes. Clearly, at this rate he was going to have to buy a whole lot more!

'Fancy company? If I change her quickly, could I come, too? And afterwards, if you were feeling really kind, you could point me in the direction of the nearest supermarket or baby shop so I can buy her more stuff.'

'Sure. I was going to walk, but we can take the

car. I'll give Georgie a ring and warn her we might be late.'

He nodded, took the baby from her gingerly and went through the fence. She was starting to fuss, but she settled once he'd changed her and put her in the carrier, and he met Emily on the drive just as she was putting Freddie into his seat.

'Can we squeeze this in?'

'This?' she said with a chuckle, taking the carrier from him. 'Poor baby, what a way to talk about you! He's a bad daddy.'

She hoisted it into the car and strapped it in, then got behind the wheel. He slid in beside her, shifting so he could watch her. 'So where are we going?'

'A friend's—actually, Georgie Cauldwell. Do you remember her? Her father's a builder—we used to go and crawl around on the building sites when we were kids.'

He nodded. 'I remember her—small but fiery. Brown hair, green eyes, lots of personality?'

She shot him a look. 'You do remember her. Very well. Did you have a thing about her, Harry?'

He laughed softly. 'Hardly. You were more than enough trouble for me.' He looked away. 'So what's she doing now?'

'She's married to a guy from London with pots of money. He's a darling. They've got three kids that were his sister's, but she was killed on the way home from hospital when she had the last one. It was awful. Anyway, they've adopted them and Georgie's pregnant now, so it's just as well they've got this big house.'

She swung into the drive of a huge Victorian villa overlooking the sea and cut the engine. Two boys came running over with a little girl he knew instantly must be Beth. She was every inch her mother's daughter, from the soft dark curls that tumbled round her shoulders to the twinkling, mischievous eyes that reminded him so much of Em when he'd first met her.

And behind them came Georgie, older of course but still essentially the same, a baby in her arms. He unfolded himself from the seat and stood up, and with a little cry of welcome she hugged him with her free arm, her smile open and friendly.

'Harry! Emily said you were back—oh, it's so good to see you again. Welcome back to Yoxburgh. Come on in and meet Nick—Oh, and this is the baby!' she added, peering into the car. 'Oh, Harry, she's lovely!'

The baby in her arms was pretty gorgeous, too, and when she burrowed her head in her mother's shoulder and then peeped at him and giggled, he couldn't help responding. 'So who's this?' he asked after a moment or two of pee-boo-ing and giggles.

'Maya,' Georgie said. 'Aren't you? She can say her name now. Tell Harry who you are.'

'Harry,' the baby said, swivelling round and pointing, and burrowed into her shoulder again. Still smiling, he followed the direction she'd pointed in and met a challenging stare.

'You've got my name,' the boy said, his head tilting to one side. 'I'm Harry.'

Harry grinned. 'Is that right?'

He nodded.

'Well, in that case I think you must have my name, since I had it about twenty something years before you needed it, but hey, that's cool, I don't mind sharing. It's a good name, it would be mean to keep it to myself.'

They swapped grins, and then he was introduced to Dickon, Harry's younger brother, and Em's daughter Beth.

So many children—and now it was his turn. He got the carrier out of the car, turned it towards them all and said with a curious feeling of rightness, 'This is Kizzy. She's my daughter.'

'Is Emily her mummy?' Dickon asked, puzzled, and Harry shook his head.

Should he say this? Hell, these kids had lost their mother only a year or so ago. Was it really fair to dredge it all up?

Yes. Because life wasn't fair, and the truth

would come out at some point, he was sure, so he shook his head again and said gently, 'Her mother died.'

'Our mummy's dead,' Dickon said matter-of-factly. 'Georgie's our new mummy. Is Emily going to be Kizzy's new mummy?'

Emily laughed, the sound a little strained to his ears, and started towards the house. 'Heavens, no! I've got enough on my plate with Beth and Freddie, haven't I, darling?'

Beth slipped her hand into her mother's and snuggled closer. 'Babies are nice, though. Georgie's having a baby.'

'Well, I'm not,' Em said firmly. Too firmly? He didn't know. All he knew was that all this blatant fecundity should have sent him running—and it didn't. And the idea of Emily being Kizzy's new mummy was suddenly extraordinarily appealing…

'Lovely house.'

Nick looked around and smiled the smile of a

supremely contented man. 'It is, isn't it? Georgie and her father did the work for us, and we love it. I thought it was ridiculously big at first, but with all the kids and another on the way and my mother living with us and working here, and me working from home at first, frankly if it was any smaller it wouldn't be big enough.'

For a man who'd evidently been a bachelor a little more than a year ago, he seemed extraordinarily happy with the way things had turned out. They were in the garden, sitting in the shade of a big old tree and looking out over the sea, and every few seconds his eyes would stray to his family, an indulgent smile touching his mouth.

Harry could understand that. His own eyes kept straying to Em and her children, her revelation about their father still ringing in his ears.

He walked—well, ran, actually. I haven't seen lightning move so fast.

Bastard. Fancy leaving them. Although maybe it had been better to leave them with Emily who clearly adored them than to stay and make them feel unloved and unwanted, and then at the first opportunity pack them off to boarding school and to their grandparents in the holidays...

'So where are you staying? Georgie said something about your grandmother's house.'

He wrenched himself back to the present and gave a rueful smile. 'Well, that was the idea, but it's had tenants since she died ten years ago and I haven't been back since the funeral. To be honest, it was a bit of a shock, seeing it. The agents told me it needed some cosmetic attention, but I think they were erring on the kind side. It needs gutting, frankly, so I think we'll have to rent something.'

Georgie lifted her head and frowned at him. 'Is it really that bad?'

'It needs total redecoration, and if I'm going to live there long term it'll need a new kitchen and bathroom at least, but for now a lick of paint and some clean carpets would work wonders. I don't suppose your father knows anyone reliable?'

Her eyes flicked to her husband's. 'We could send in the A-team.'

Nick chuckled. 'Indeed. We've got a whole range of trades,' he explained. 'They're used to working together, they do a good job, their prices are reasonable and at the moment they're not busy because there's been a hold-up on a development. So—yeah, if you want, we could send them along to give you a quote.'

'Fantastic. That would be great.'

And if they could do half at a time, he could stay there. It was summer, after all, and he and the baby could spend most of their time in the garden.

He didn't let himself think too much about why it seemed so important to stay there rather than rent another house—one that wouldn't be next to Em. After all, she'd already made it clear she wasn't interested in being Kizzy's new mummy.

Not that he was about to ask her, or had even really thought about it for more than a moment, but he thought about it now—couldn't think about anything else, in fact, however foolish he knew it was. If he had any sense he'd keep well out of her way and not indulge the foolish fantasy that they, too, could have a fairy tale ending like Georgie and Nick…

Emily was stunned.

If I'm going to live there long term?

He was considering it? Really?

She'd thought he was back for a few days—just a quick visit to sort out the house ready for the next tenants. It had never occurred to her that he might be coming back for any length of time—or maybe even for good!

But if he *was* back for good—no. She couldn't let herself think about it. Daren't let herself think about it, because her heart couldn't take any more. She'd been stupid over Harry Kavenagh once too often, and she wasn't going to do it again.

'So when can you start?'

'Tomorrow? We'll strip all the wallpaper and

rip out the old floorcoverings, decorate throughout and then you'll be ready for the new carpets. Should take a week at the most with the team on it.'

'A week?'

'Uh-huh. Some of the windows need quite a bit of work, unless you're going to replace them?'

'Um—I hadn't intended to. I was hoping to live here while you do it.'

'With the baby?' The foreman shook his head. 'No. Sorry, I really wouldn't recommend it. Not with all the old lead paint. It's OK when it's left alone, but when it's disturbed it can be harmful to children, and she's so tiny.' His face softened as he looked down at the baby in Harry's arms, and Harry's eyes followed his gaze and his eyes locked with Kizzy's.

Wide and trusting, fixed on him.

'No, you're right,' he said, wondering what on earth he did now. 'Come tomorrow. I'll find somewhere to go. It's not like there's much here to worry about in the way of furnishings. I'll get carpets and stuff organised for when it's done, so it won't be for long.'

He waved them off, hesitated on the doorstep and then went round to Emily's house and rang the doorbell.

'Oh. It's you,' she said, wondering if there would ever come a time when her heart didn't hiccup at the sight of him. 'I thought you would have come through the fence and knocked on the back door.'

He smiled a little awkwardly. 'I don't want to take advantage.'

'You aren't taking advantage.' She opened the door a little wider. 'Come on in. I was just about to have coffee. Join me.'

'Thanks.' He followed her down the hall and into the kitchen, perching on the stool awkwardly with Kizzy snuggled against his chest, and watched her while she made their drinks.

'Still off coffee?' she asked with a smile, and he shook his head, his mouth kicking up in an answering smile.

'No. I need caffeine today. I've just had the decorator round. He's coming tomorrow, but they're going to hit the whole house at once and strip it all right out. I need to find a hotel for us for a week. I wondered if you'd got any ideas or recommendations?'

'A hotel?' she said, and then, knowing she was going to do it and utterly unable to stop her mouth making the words, she said, 'Don't be silly. You can stay here. It's only a week. You'll be no trouble.'

No trouble? Was she out of her mind? And what was she thinking, *only* a week? That was seven nights! Well, five if she was lucky and he was talking working weeks, but it was Monday now, and if they'd said it would take a week then there'd be a weekend in between and so it would be properly a week before the decorators left, and then the carpets would have to be fitted and the furniture delivered. So, next Wednesday at the earliest. Oh, rats. Still, the house was plenty big enough and there were three bathrooms. They wouldn't be tripping over each other at least.

Besides, it was too late, because he was accepting, hesitantly, reluctantly, but still accepting, and only a real bitch would say, 'Actually, no, I've changed my mind, I didn't mean it at all!'

Or a woman whose life was complicated enough, whose heart was finding it altogether too difficult to be so close to the person who'd held that heart in the palm of his hand for so very many years…

'I've found my old baby sling,' she told him, putting the coffee down in front of him and lifting the sling off the end of the worktop where she'd put it ready to give him.

'Baby sling?'

She smiled and handed it to him. 'You put it round your shoulders and over your back, and the baby lies against your front, without you having to hold her all the time, so she can hear your heart beat and you have your hands free. They're wonderful.'

He studied the little heap of soft stretchy cotton fabric with interest. 'I've seen things like this all over the world—women tying their babies to them so they can work, either on their fronts so they can feed them easily, or on their backs.'

She nodded. 'The so-called civilised West has just cottoned on. It's a big thing now. They call it baby-wearing, as if they'd just invented it, but since you seem to be doing it anyway I thought you might like to borrow that to make it easier.'

'Thanks. You'll have to give me lessons,' he said, putting it down again with a defeated laugh. 'It looks like a loop of fabric to me.'

'It is. Here.'

And just because it was easier to show him than to put it on him with the baby still in his arms, she looped it round herself, adjusted it, took the baby from him and snuggled her inside it, close against her heart.

Kizzy shifted, sighed and snuggled closer, relaxing back into sleep without a murmur. 'See? Then you get your hands free.'

He gave a cheeky, crooked grin. 'Or I could let you carry her, since you seem to be the expert.'

She laughed, sat down and sipped her coffee, relishing the feel of the little one against her, warm and curiously reassuring. No. She mustn't let herself get too used to it. It was much, much too dangerous. Her heart had already been broken by this man, and there was no way she was going to let his daughter do the same thing.

'I don't suppose you want to come carpet shopping with me?'

She met his eyes over her cup. 'Can't you cope?' she asked, desperately trying to create a little distance, and then could have kicked herself because she would have loved to go carpet shopping with him.

He shrugged dismissively. 'Of course I can cope. I just thought it might be more fun.'

'What, with Freddie in tow and Mini-Dot here yelling the place down? I don't think so.'

'She's not yelling now,' he pointed out. 'Maybe she's stopped that.'

Foolish, foolish man.

The baby began to stir almost before he'd finished speaking, and within seconds she was bawling her tiny lungs out.

'I'll get her bottle,' he said, standing up, but Emily got up, too, extracted Kizzy from the sling and handed her to him.

'I've got a better idea. You take her and deal with her, and when she's settled, you can take her carpet shopping. And I can get on with my work.'

A fleeting frown crossed his brow. 'I'm sorry. I didn't realise you were working,' he said, and took Kizzy from her arms. 'We'll get out of your way. And don't worry about having us to stay. We'll find a hotel.'

'Harry, no!' she said, angry with herself for upsetting him.

'No, really,' he said, his voice a little gruff. 'I'm sorry. I can't just come back here after all these years and expect you to welcome me with open arms.'

Oh, Harry, if you only knew, she thought, and

her hand came out and curled over his wrist, holding him there with her. 'I didn't mean it like that. It's just—I do have work to do, and Freddie is having a nap and it's my one chance. Please, come and stay. I can't let you go to a hotel. Not with the baby. Anyway, Freddie and Beth will love having her here. Please?'

His eyes were serious, searching hers for an endless moment, and then, finally satisfied, he nodded briefly. 'OK. But we'll try and keep out of your way so we don't stop you working.'

She felt the tension go out of her like air out of a balloon. 'Still want help with the carpet shopping?' she said with a smile.

CHAPTER THREE

HE HADN'T realised just what an expedition it would be, shopping with three children.

Kizzy was more than enough trouble, but by the time he'd got her fed and settled and Freddie had woken up, Beth had come back from playing with a friend, so they were all going together.

And then, of course, because she was so tiny and seemed to be hungry every three minutes or so, he needed to take feeds for Kizzy, and because she was just like a straw he'd need nappies, and because he was so rubbish at putting the nappies on she'd need a total change of clothes…

He bet they took less equipment on an Arctic expedition.

'You OK there?'

He gave Emily what he hoped was a smile and nodded. 'Sure. I'm fine. I've got everything, I think.'

She eyed the bulging bag dubiously. 'Got wipes?'

Of course not.

He found them and put them in, then straightened up, baby carrier in hand. 'Will I need the sling? Because I still don't think I know how to put it on.'

'I'll help you. Bring it,' she instructed, and so he followed her out—to her car, not his, because it was set up with baby seats for her two. Beth and Freddie were already strapped in, reaching across and poking each other and giggling, and they looked up and beamed a welcome at him and Kizzy that made him feel—just for a second, until he reminded himself that he wasn't—as if he was a part of their family.

As if he belonged.

And the pain hit him in the chest like a sledgehammer.

He sucked in a breath. 'Hi, kids,' he said, leaning over Freddie to put the baby carrier in the middle, and Freddie reached up and grabbed his face and planted a wet, sticky kiss on his cheek.

'Harry!' he said happily, and Harry straightened up and ruffled Freddie's hair and swallowed hard.

No. They weren't his kids. He wasn't going to get involved. Look what had happened the last time he'd got involved in someone's life...

'All set?'

He clipped on his seat belt and nodded. Emily started the car and headed for town.

It was a good job he had her in tow, she thought.

He was fingering a lovely pale pure wool carpet with a thoughtful look on his face.

'Imagine it with baby sick and play-dough on it,' she advised sagely, and he wrinkled his nose and sighed heavily.

'So what would you suggest?'

'Something a little darker? Something scrubbable? There are some you can pour bleach on. Maybe a tiny pattern, just to break it up? Or a heather mix, so it's not a flat, plain colour.'

He was glazing over, she could tell. Poor baby. For the first time in his life he was up against having to consider something other than his own taste. And he didn't like it.

'I want wood, really. I'd like to strip the boards, or put down an oak strip floor, perhaps. I've got solid walnut in my flat and it's gorgeous. And you can wipe it clean.'

'Hard to fall on, and it can be a bit cold. Anyway, they probably couldn't do a really nice floor that fast.'

'Oh, damn,' he said, ramming his hands through his hair and grinning ruefully. 'I tell you what, you choose. You've had more experience than I have. So long as it covers the floor and I can have it next Tuesday, I don't care.'

So she chose—a soft pale coffee mix that would stand children running in and out—and then wondered what on earth she was thinking about because the only child running in and out would be Kizzy and she was less than two weeks old! He'd probably replace the carpet before she was walking.

'Next?'

'Furniture? I haven't got any.'

So she took him to a place that sold beds and sofas and dining furniture, and he ordered the best compromise between what he wanted and what was available at short notice, and then right on cue Kizzy started up.

Freddie was wriggling around in the buggy, wanting to get out, and Beth was hanging on her hand and needed the loo.

'How about lunch?' she suggested. 'Then we can tackle curtains and bedding—a bit more retail therapy for you.'

'Retail therapy?' He gave a snort. 'Not in this lifetime—but lunch sounds good,' he said, the air of hunted desperation easing slightly at the suggestion of reprieve, and she nearly laughed out loud.

Poor Harry. Anyone less in touch with their feminine side she had yet to meet, but she had to hand it to him. He was taking it on the chin and giving it his best shot, and she felt a strangely proprietorial sense of pride in him.

Swallowing a lump in her throat, Emily tucked her arm through his and steered him into the little café next door, sat him and Beth down, found a high chair for Freddie and took Kizzy from the sling on Harry's chest, rocking her while the waitress heated the bottle. Then she fed her while her children played with their bendy straws and Harry sat back and closed his eyes and inhaled a double espresso with the air of a condemned man taking his last meal.

It was all she could do not to laugh.

'Well, that was painless.'

'Painless?' He cracked an eye open and studied her for signs of lunacy. 'I thought we'd never get them settled. I'm exhausted.'

'You'll get used to it,' she promised. 'I did.'

'You're a woman. You have hormones.'

'Yes—and usually they're a hazard,' she said with a chuckle in her voice, and he opened the other eye and sat up a little.

They were in her sitting room, all three children sound asleep, and his few possessions were now installed in Dan's bedroom, which just happened to be next to hers. Unfortunately. He could have done with being at the other end of the hall, or downstairs, or even at the end of the garden—

No. He couldn't afford to think about the summerhouse. Not now, when he was alone with her for the first time in years, and there was soft music flowing all around them and all he wanted to do was take her in his arms and carry on where they'd left off…

'Are you OK?'

'Sure. Why?'

'You're scowling.'

He tried to iron out the muscles in his face and struggled for a smile. 'Sorry. Thanks for today.

I don't suppose you enjoyed it any more than I did,' he said, and then realised it was actually a lie, because in some bizarre way he had enjoyed it, all of it. And because he couldn't lie to her, because he never had, he shook his head and smiled again, properly this time. 'Actually, it was fun, in a strange way,' he admitted, and she smiled back, her eyes soft with understanding.

'You'll get used to it, Harry. It's not so bad after a while.'

'Because it's so long since you've done anything for yourself that you forget to miss it?' he suggested, and she gave a wry chuckle.

'Got it in one. And the kids are lovely. They give you back all that love in spades.'

He studied her, wondering about her love life, if it consisted solely of cuddles with her adorable children or if there was a man somewhere.

'You're scowling again.'

He laughed. 'Sorry. Tell me about your garden design business. Did you do your parents' garden? I noticed it was different—better.'

'Do you like it? I did it years ago. It was one of my first projects. The swing seat had broken, and the garden needed a thorough overhaul. My father asked me if I wanted to do it as my first commission, when I was finishing my course. I would have done it anyway, but he insisted on paying me—said I had to live and he was sick of supporting me!'

Harry laughed with her, picturing her father, gruff and loving, always supportive, and her mother, warm and motherly and generous to a fault, like a younger version of his grandmother Grace.

'You're very lucky to have such loving parents,' he said, his own voice a little gruff, and she nodded, her eyes searching his face and missing nothing, he was sure. He looked away. 'So how's business now?'

'Good,' she said. 'I've done quite a bit for Nick and Georgie, both in their garden and in the development behind their house, and Nick's got some other projects under way that I'm drawing up some ideas for, and I've done a few other domestic jobs around the area.'

'Enough to live on?'

'I manage,' she said, but there was something in her voice that made him wonder how tight it was and how dependent she was on her parents for accommodation, or if it simply suited them all. He wondered if the rat who'd fathered her children and then legged it made any kind of contribution, and thought probably not.

'No, he doesn't,' she said, and his head jerked up.

'Did I say that out loud?' he said guiltily, but she shook her head, her smile wry.

'No. You didn't have to. You were scowling again.'

'Ah.' He pressed his lips together, but the words came out anyway. 'Tell me about him.'

She shrugged. 'Nothing to tell. I met him at a party—no surprises there. He's always been a party animal. We lived together for a year, and I became pregnant with Beth. He wanted

me to get rid of her, as he put it, but I wouldn't.
I told him it was too late, and I really thought
he'd come to love her, but he was pretty indif-
ferent to her.'

'So why didn't you leave him?'

Her laugh was humourless and a little bitter.
'I had nothing to live on. I didn't think it was fair
to come home to my parents. They were
enjoying being free of responsibility, and they
were taking all the holidays they couldn't afford
while Dan and I were at home. So I stayed with
Pete, and two years later I was pregnant again.'

'And he left you.'

'Mmm. I told him on Saturday morning, and
on Saturday afternoon he packed up and moved
out while I was at the supermarket. He left me
with the flat, the rent was due and I had no
money for food. He'd stopped my card so I
couldn't use it at the supermarket, and when I
got home with no food after an embarrassing
fiasco at the checkout, he was gone.'

'So what did you do?'

'I came home. My father collected us and brought us home, my mother looked after Beth so I could go back to work until I had Freddie, and they've been fantastic. I don't know what I would have done without them.'

Her voice was soft and matter-of-fact, but underneath he could sense a wealth of pain and he ached for her. He knew what it was to be unwanted, knew how it felt to be an unwanted child, and having heard her story he was more than ever sure that Beth and Freddie were better off without their father.

'You don't need him,' he said, and she smiled.

'I know. And you don't have to sound so cross. He did me a favour, really. Without him I wouldn't have had my children, and at least he had the decency to go off and leave us alone, instead of hanging around and being cruel...'

He felt his legs bunch. 'He hit you?'

She laughed and shook her head, leaning over to push him back onto the sofa. 'Relax. There are other ways of being cruel.'

Oh, yes. And he'd met many of them in his time. He relaxed back against the sofa and sighed, then patted the cushion beside him. 'Come here.'

She hesitated a second, then she sat beside him, snuggling against his side as she'd done so very many times before. 'I've missed you,' she said softly. 'I see you on the telly and wonder how you are, if you'll ever come back to Suffolk…'

'And I have.'

'Mmm. With Kizzy. I might have known you'd find a waif and rescue her. You were always a softie.'

He thought of Carmen, how she'd looked after she'd been attacked, and how she'd looked in the chapel at the mortuary, her young face finally at peace.

'I don't think I did her any favours,' he said gruffly. 'Maybe if I'd left her there, or handed her over to the aid agencies…'

'Then what? She would have had a child and

no way of supporting it except prostitution. Would you want that for her?'

He shook his head. 'But she didn't deserve to die.'

'Of course not, but life's a bitch, Harry. You gave her hope, gave her a home—and you've given her baby a home and a father, safety and security for the rest of her life.'

'We have yet to survive it, of course,' he said wryly. 'Only time will tell.'

'You'll survive it.' She tipped up her face and smiled at him, her hand coming up to cradle his jaw with gentle fingers. 'You'll be a wonderful father, Harry. Give yourself time.'

He nodded slightly, not sure if he could believe her but no longer really thinking about it, because her eyes were tender, her mouth was full and soft and, oh, so close, and without thinking, without giving himself time to analyse or argue or reason, he lowered his head and touched his lips to hers.

Oh, dear heaven, she tasted the same. All these years and he could remember her taste, her scent, the feel of her lips under his, the soft stroke of her tongue against his, the tiny sigh, the warmth of her breath, the frantic beating of her heart against his fingertips as his hand glided down over the hollow of her throat and settled against a soft, full breast, fuller than before, her body a woman's now, lush and generous, the curves just right for his hand.

And he wanted her as he had never wanted her before, as an adult, a man who knew all the joys in store instead of a hormonal youth who simply hoped to find out. And the knowledge was almost enough to destroy his self-control, to push him over the edge.

But then, just as he was about to let her go, when his mind was already pulling back even as his hand curled against her breast, she lifted her head away, her eyes confused, and said, 'Kizzy.'

Kizzy? What had Kizzy to do with it?

And then he heard her crying, her screams getting louder by the second.

He jerked himself to his feet, strode towards

the door and bounded upstairs, his heart racing and his body clamouring to turn round and go back and finish what they'd started…

Emily sagged back against the cushions and lifted her hand to her lips. Had it really always felt that good? And if so, how on earth had they ever stopped?

She closed her eyes and waited for her heart to slow, listening to his voice, a soft rumble on the stairs as he carried Kizzy down. Her cries subsided for the moment, a cuddle enough to comfort her for now.

Emily nearly laughed aloud. A cuddle from Kizzy's father was nothing like enough to comfort her. She wanted more—much more—but she'd be insane to let this crazy situation go any further, because whatever else she knew about Harry, she knew that Yoxburgh wouldn't be enough to satisfy him for long.

He'd always talked about seeing the world—a result of his restless upbringing, trailing round the globe in the wake of his parents who had been too busy to pay attention to their little son. So although he'd never had their love, he'd had experiences in spades, and the wanderlust that was a part of his father's make up was part of his also.

And so he'd go—maybe not now, maybe not for a while, but eventually, when it all got too dull and easy and the world beckoned. And she'd be left, broken-hearted as Pete could never have left her, because although she'd thought she'd loved Pete, she knew full well that an affair with Harry had the potential to bring her far more joy and far more sorrow than Pete could ever have done, because he'd never had that unerring capacity to touch her soul.

So she simply wasn't going to go there, not now, not ever. And if they'd got scarily close on the night of his grandmother's funeral, they weren't getting that close again. No way. It was far too dangerous.

She could hear him in the kitchen, hear Kizzy starting up again, and taking a deep breath to steady her, she got to her feet and went through. 'Want a hand?'

'I'm OK,' he said, his back to her and his voice tight.

Damn.

'I'm going to do some work, then,' she said, and went into the study and shut the door a little more firmly than was quite necessary, just to be on the safe side.

'Oh, Kizzy, what did I go and do that for?' he murmured, staring down at his tiny daughter with regret. 'We were getting on so well, and now I've gone and screwed everything up, but she was just there, you know, and I just wanted to kiss her. Nothing else. What a silly daddy.'

He took the bottle out of her mouth and propped her up against his shoulder, rubbing her back until she burped gloriously in his ear, then he gave her the rest of the bottle, cuddled her for a minute and then took her back up, changed her and put her down in the travel cot Em had found in the loft.

Kizzy went out like a light, without a murmur, which left him nothing to do but go back downstairs and sit and watch the study door and wonder if Emily was mad with him.

He paused in Freddie's doorway, staring down at the sleeping boy. He was huge compared to Kizzy, but he was still a baby really, his steps sometimes unsteady, his chin only too ready to wobble if things went wrong. Beth wasn't that much older, either, but quite different, bright and beautiful and full of mischief, her sparkling eyes just like Em's.

Beth was lying sprawled across the bed, too close to the edge, and he shifted her back and covered her again before heading downstairs with all the enthusiasm of a French aristo going to the guillotine.

He owed Em an apology, and he wasn't sure if he dared be in the room with her long enough to make it. At least not without a table between them to keep them apart.

He went into the kitchen, made some tea and tapped on the study door. 'Em?'

'Come in,' she said, turning towards him with a wary look in her eyes as he pushed the door open and went in, tray in hand.

'I've brought you tea.'

'Thanks.'

He hung on to the tray, because if it was in his hands he couldn't do anything else with them. 'My pleasure. And we haven't eaten. Want me to cook something?'

She swivelled her chair a little farther and reached for the tea. 'What can you cook?'

He laughed. 'Probably nothing English. What have you got to work with?'

'All sorts. I did a big shop the other day. Go and have a look. I just want to finish this off and I'll come and give you a hand.'

He nodded and went out, sighing with relief that the awkwardness seemed to have gone and their friendship was back on track.

Unless he poisoned her! He opened the fridge

and studied the contents. Peppers, chicken breast, onions, tiny cherry tomatoes, salad, apples in the fruit bowl, couscous in the larder cupboard and spices in the rack next to the hob.

Excellent.

'Smells good.'

He jumped, turning towards her with a laugh lighting up his eyes and the knife pointing towards her threateningly, but she didn't feel threatened. 'Do you have to creep up on me?'

'Sorry.' She grinned without remorse and perched on the stool at the breakfast bar. 'Found all you need?'

'I think so. Did you get your drawing done?'

'Yes. I was just making a few changes to the planting. So what are you cooking?'

'Moroccan chicken and couscous. I wasn't sure if you liked things spicy, so I haven't made it too hot, but it's fruity so it takes the edge off it. Here—try a bit.'

And he held out a fork with a little pile of

couscous on for her to taste. She leant forward, closed her lips around the fork and wondered if he'd been tasting it, if his lips had closed on the prongs of the fork, too, if he'd…

'Wow! That's gorgeous!'

'Not too hot for you?'

She shook her head, putting her hormones back in their box and concentrating on the food. 'No, it's lovely.'

'Good. I'll just finish off the chicken and I'll be done.'

'Want a hand?'

'No. Just stay there and keep me company.'

So she sat there, watching him work, her eyes drawn to the muscles in his shoulders flexing as he stirred and flipped the chicken in the pan, his buttocks taut when he shifted from foot to foot, crouching to lift out the plates from the oven and then straightening, thighs working…

Damn. She was going to drool in a minute.

He threw the chicken into the couscous, scraped the juices into the mixture and stirred it through then piled it into the bowls and set them down on the breakfast bar in front of her, hooking his foot round a stool and drawing it closer before sitting opposite her.

Their knees brushed and she pulled away, just as he did, and he apologised automatically and then he met her eyes and smiled wryly. 'Actually, I'm sorry for all of it. For landing on you like this—for kissing you.' Then he shook his head and laughed softly under his breath. 'No, that's a lie. I'm not sorry. I'm sorry I'm not sorry, if you see what I mean. I didn't mean to kiss you, and I shouldn't have done, but I can't be sorry I did. Not unless it gets in the way of our friendship, because that means too much to me to mess with it. Ah, that was the most garbled speech in the world, but—I guess what I'm trying to say is, forgive me?'

Forgive him? For kissing her so tenderly, so beautifully, so skillfully?

'There's nothing to forgive,' she said, her

voice a little unsteady, and picking up her fork, she turned her attention to the food before she said or did anything she'd regret…

CHAPTER FOUR

'CAN I ask you an enormous favour?'

Emily lifted her eyes from the baby's face and met Harry's clear blue gaze. Maybe one day she'd be immune to watching him with the baby in his arms as he fed her, but not today or any time soon.

'Sure,' she said, wondering if her voice was as husky as she suspected.

'I need to go to London. I didn't really give them much warning that I was going to be taking time off. I'll go on the train, I think it's the quickest, and I shouldn't be gone more than five hours—six, tops. I'll leave all the feeds ready for you—the made-up packets are a doddle, even I can manage them, and with any luck she'll sleep for most of it, but I need to go and talk to my boss, and I can't really take her with me.'

'Why not?' she suggested, just to see what he said and to find out if he'd thought it through. 'It might be quite useful—you know, make the point of how tiny she is and all that.'

He shook his head, his mouth kicking up in a wry smile. 'No. My boss is a woman. There's no way she'd be impressed by that. She'd expect a woman to get child care to cover a meeting. She won't make an exception for me. And I know it's a pain, and I promise I won't make a habit of it. It's really just this once. And, yes, I could take her and dump her on a secretary or something on the way in, but it isn't really fair on the secretary and it certainly isn't fair on Kizzy. I've already thought about doing it, and if I didn't have to ask you, I wouldn't. I know you've got more than enough to do, and I'll make it up to you—babysit yours so you can get some work done or something. Look after them while you get a massage. Whatever you like.'

She put him out of his misery. 'Done. You can babysit for me while I work, *and* I'll have a massage. And you can pay for it,' she added, waiting for him to renege, but he didn't, he just nodded and looked relieved.

'Thanks, Em. I owe you.'

'I know. The meter's running.'

He chuckled and lifted the baby against his shoulder, burping her. Hell, he was getting good at it. Those big strong hands cradled her with a tenderness that made Emily want to weep, and now he was relaxing into the role, Kizzy obviously felt safe. Emily envied her. She'd give her eye teeth to be cradled in his arms with him staring adoringly down at her like that.

She shot to her feet. 'More tea?'

He shook his head. 'No, I'm going to turn in. I'm shattered. So—is that OK for the morning, then?'

'Tomorrow?' she said, startled, and he nodded.

'Sorry—didn't I mention that? Is tomorrow a problem?'

'No,' she said, mentally scanning her diary. 'Except the decorators are starting.'

'Hell,' he said softly. 'Could you keep an eye on them? Make sure they're OK and don't do anything silly?'

'Have you agreed colours?'

'Colours?' He looked suddenly overwhelmed, and she took pity on him. He'd had a hard day, and the learning curve must seem to him as steep as Everest.

'Don't worry. I expect they'll be doing preparation for a day or two. I'll pick up some colour charts for you, or they might have some. If all else fails I'll decide for you—but don't blame me if you come back and find the hall sore-throat pink!'

'You wouldn't,' he said, his eyes filled with panic, and she chuckled.

'Don't push your luck. Go on, go to bed and we'll sort the rest out in the morning.'

He nodded and stood up, the baby asleep in the crook of his arm, and he paused beside her and looked down into her eyes. The light was behind him so she couldn't read his expression, but his voice was gruff.

'You're a star, Em. I don't know what I would have done without you.'

And without warning he bent his head and brushed his lips lightly against hers, then with a murmured, 'Good night.' He went upstairs and left her there, still reeling from his touch...

The overhead lines were down.

He couldn't believe it. He'd had the day from hell. His boss had grilled him like a kipper about when he was going to be able to return to work, he'd had his contract terms pointed out to him in words of one syllable, his mobile phone battery had died and now this.

The train had come to a shuddering halt midway between stations, and there was nothing they could do but wait for the lines to be repaired. And in the meantime the air-conditioning was out of action because the train wasn't running, and the staff were wandering up and down, handing out bottled water and reassurance while the entire world got on the phone and told their loved ones what was going on.

Except him. Because his battery was flat, because with everything else he'd had to do he'd forgotten to put it on charge. And now Em wouldn't know where he was or be able to get hold of him, and some woman next to him had recognised him and was hell-bent on making conversation. He would have borrowed her mobile and phoned Em, but her number was in his phone so he couldn't get it and besides he didn't want the number registered on the woman's call log, because there was just something persistent about her that rang alarm bells.

So he sat, stripped down to his shirtsleeves and wondering if it would be rude to take off his shoes and socks, and endured her conversation in the sweltering heat and worried about Kizzy and whether Em was coping, until he could have screamed.

* * *

Where *was* he?

She looked at her watch again, and tried his mobile once more, just in case, but either he was stuck in the underground, it was switched off or the battery was dead.

And Kizzy was refusing her feeds. She'd been sick, she'd spent most of the afternoon with her legs bent up, screaming, and finally Em had got Freddie and Beth off to bed and was pacing up and down, Kizzy in her arms turned against her front for comfort, and she was grizzling and hiccupping and it was tearing Emily apart.

She shifted her from one arm to the other because she was getting cramp, but as she settled her on the other side her breast brushed Kizzy's cheek and she turned her little head, instinctively rooting for the nipple.

And with her maternal instinct kicking in, Emily's nipples started to prickle and bead with milk, even though it had been months since she'd given up feeding Freddie.

Months and months, but as far as her body was

concerned it could have been yesterday, and she pressed the heel of her hand against the other breast and bit her lips to hold back a whimper.

Oh, she ached to feed her. The instinct was overwhelming, and Kizzy felt it, too, nuzzling her and sobbing, and in the end it was more than she could bear.

How could it hurt? Wetnursing had been around for ever—for as long as mothers had died in childbirth, other women had fed their babies for them, and no one had thought twice about it. It was only now, in this sanitised age where bottle-feeding was an accepted option that anyone would even blink at the idea.

And anyway, she didn't need food, she needed comfort, poor motherless little scrap, and if Emily could provide comfort for this tragic infant, then who was she to deny it?

She sat down in the middle of the sofa, unfastened her bra and lifted it out of the way, then turned the baby to her nipple, brushing it against her cheek, and as if she'd been doing it all her life, Kizzy turned to her, opened her mouth and latched on.

There. Just like that, peace was restored. The hiccupping sobs faded to nothing, the only sound in the room was the rhythmic suckling of the baby, and cradling her close, Emily stroked the back of the tiny starfish hand pressed against her breast and closed her eyes.

Poor baby. She should have done it hours ago, but she'd thought Harry would be back.

She glanced at her watch, concerned for him. The decorators had been and gone, leaving colour charts behind, and she'd made them tea and chatted over the fence in between feeds and Freddie's tantrums and Beth's persistent demands for attention, and somehow the day had disappeared.

Now it was night, almost eight-thirty, and it was getting dark outside.

She was just about to phone him again when she heard a key in the door. She felt a sudden flutter of panic, and glanced down at Kizzy.

What if he was angry? What if he didn't understand? She thought of prising the baby off and reassembling her clothes, but there wasn't time, and anyway, she couldn't lie to him. She'd have to tell him, whatever, and she'd just have to hope he could understand.

'Em, I'm so sorry—the wires were down…'

He trailed to a halt, staring in amazement. She was *suckling* her! Breastfeeding Kizzy, as if it was the most natural thing in the world, and he felt a huge lump clog his throat.

For a moment he couldn't move, but then his legs kicked in again, and crossing over to her, he hunkered down and reached out a finger, stroking the baby's head, then looked up into Emily's stricken eyes. 'You're feeding her,' he said hoarsely.

'I'm sorry. She wouldn't settle—she's been crying for hours, and it seemed the only sensible thing to do. I'm really sorry, it's the only time—'

'Sorry?' He stared at her in astonishment. 'For

giving her what her poor mother was unable to give her? Emily, no. Don't be sorry. She had donated milk in SCBU, just to start her off, but of course I couldn't keep it up. Don't have the equipment.' He smiled, and then his smile wobbled a bit and he frowned. 'I just— It was the one thing I couldn't do for her, the one thing I've felt so really bad about, and I never thought for a moment, never dreamt—'

He broke off, choked, and rested a trembling hand on Kizzy's head, watching as her damp little mouth worked at Em's nipple, and a surge of emotion washed over him, so strong it would have taken the legs out from under him if he hadn't already been down there.

'You couldn't get me a drink, could you?' she said, her voice soft, and he nodded and cleared his throat.

'Yeah. Sure. Of course. What do you want?'

'Tea? I'd better not have juice, it might upset her.'

He stood up, his legs a little unsteady, and went

out to the kitchen, put the kettle on and leant his head against the wall cupboard while the world shifted back gradually onto an even keel.

He'd fantasised about this.

For the past two days, whenever she'd been carrying the baby or holding her like that, turned in to her body, he'd fantasised about her breast-feeding his child.

Not that Kizzy was his, except he couldn't imagine her being any more important to him whatever her parentage, and Em certainly wasn't his to fantasise over, but that hadn't stopped him, and now she'd brought his fantasy to life.

Only the once, he reminded himself. She'd probably never do it again, and why should she, really? It was a hell of a tie, and Kizzy was nothing to do with her. Anybody else would have shut her in a bedroom and left her to cry herself to sleep.

But not Em. His Emily had always been fiercely protective of children, breaking up squabbles on the beach when she was only ten, leading crying toddlers back to their distraught parents—he couldn't remember a time when she hadn't mothered something, be it a child or an animal.

That was the first time he'd been in the summerhouse, when she'd shown him a hedgehog with a damaged leg. She'd put it in a box in the summerhouse, and she had been feeding it on cat food bought out of her pocket money. He'd helped her look after it, and they'd both ended up with fleas.

He laughed softly at the thought, and her voice behind him caught him by surprise.

'Penny for them.'

He turned with a smile. 'I was remembering the fleas from the hedgehog you rescued. And here you've got another little stray.'

'Hopefully not with fleas.' She chuckled and handed him the baby. 'Anyway, she's your little stray and she needs her nappy changed. I'll make the tea—or do you want something else?'

A large bottle of Scotch? Nothing else would blot out the hellish day—but Emily had, with her gentle smile and her loving kindness to his daughter.

'Tea would be lovely,' he said, his voice suddenly rough, and took the baby upstairs to change her and put her in her cot. He checked the others, went back downstairs and found Em in the sitting room, the mugs on the table in front of her. She was sitting on the chair, not one of the two sofas, retreating, he imagined, to a place of safety, a place where it wouldn't be so easy for him to sit beside her, draw her into his arms and kiss her senseless.

For a second he was tempted to scoop her up out of the chair and sit down in it with her on his lap, but then common sense prevailed— better late than never—and he dropped into a corner of one of the sofas, facing her.

'Bad day?'

'Probably nearly as bad as yours,' he confessed with a wry smile.

'So how was your boss?'

His laugh sounded humourless, probably

because it was. 'Let's just say she could have been more accommodating. I've taken a month's unpaid leave to give me time to sort things out. Let's just hope it's long enough.' He picked up his tea and cradled the mug in his hand, his head resting back against the cushion and his eyes closed. 'Oh, bliss. It's good to be home,' he said, and then almost stopped breathing, because that was exactly what it had felt like—coming home.

For the first time in his adult life.

He straightened up and turned his attention to the tea. 'So how did the decorators get on?' he asked, once he was sure he could trust his voice.

'OK. They've stripped out all the old carpets and put them in a skip, and they've started work on the windows. Here, colour charts.'

She pushed a pile of charts towards him on the table, and he put down his tea and picked them up, thumbing through them. 'What do you think?'

'I have no idea. I don't know what your taste is, Harry. I haven't seen you since you were twenty one, at your grandmother's funeral. Our minds weren't on décor.'

No. They'd been on other things entirely, he remembered, and wished she hadn't brought it up, because he was straight back to the summerhouse, scene of many a moonlit tryst in their teens, stolen moments together on a voyage of discovery that now seemed so innocent and then had seemed so daring, so clandestine. Except that night, after he'd buried his grandmother, when things had got just that bit closer.

'Neutral,' he said, dragging his mind back from the brink. 'Or should children have bright primary colours to stimulate them?'

She shrugged. 'I don't know. I go with instinct, and my instinct is earth colours, unless you're talking about toys, but they can be put away and leave the place calm.'

'Calm, then.'

'I think so.'

He nodded and tried to pay attention to the

colour charts, but all he could think of was their first kiss and their last—until last night, that was, only twenty-four hours ago, and still much too fresh in his mind. Coupled with coming home—there he went again—and finding Emily feeding Kizzy, he was having a hard time keeping his mind off sex and on the subject.

No. Not sex.

Emily. Emily in his arms, Emily's lips on his, Emily holding the baby, suckling her, the image still so powerful it was going to blow his mind.

He threw the colour charts down. 'I'll look at them tomorrow. See them in context. I can't even remember what colour sofas I chose now.'

She laughed, reaching for her tea and curling back up in the chair, her legs folded so that her feet were tucked up under that lovely curve of her bottom. 'Brown,' she told him. 'Bitter chocolate in that thick, bumpy leather—the tough stuff.'

'Right.' Concentrate on the sofas. 'So shoe buckles and toys don't scratch them. I remember. So we probably don't want to paint the walls black, then.'

She laughed again, and he felt it ripple right through him. 'Probably not. So, tell me about your boss.'

He shook his head. 'She was tough—tougher than the leather. I knew she would be. Don't worry, I can deal with her. It was the journey home that was so awful. There was a woman on the train who recognised me, and I was trapped with her for hours. I was getting ready to strangle her. She was creepy. I got the feeling that if the sun set I wouldn't have been safe.'

Em spluttered with laughter. 'Was she after you, Harry?'

'I think she might have been,' he confessed drily. 'Then again it might just be paranoia.'

'Or your ego.'

'Or my ego,' he conceded with a grin. 'Yeah, she was probably just a nice woman who was bored as hell and thought she could tell me her life story because she knew me. That's the trouble with spending your evenings in everybody's living rooms—they think they know you, and I suppose to a certain extent they do. Depends how much you give away to the camera.'

She tipped her head on one side, studying him. 'How much do you give away?'

He shrugged, trying to be casual because he knew the answer was that he gave away too much of himself, even if it didn't show on camera. 'Depends. As little as possible, but sometimes things really get to you—like the earthquakes and the mudslides and things. Hideous. You can't keep that under wraps. Not if you're human. And then there are the fantastic moments when they pull a child out alive days later—I can't just tell it deadpan, but you have to bear in mind you're reporting the news and not making a social commentary. That's not my job, and if I have feelings or allegiances, I have to ignore them. It's all about being impartial, about giving people the facts and letting them make their own minds up. So I try not to give my own feelings away, but sometimes—well, sometimes I fail.'

He laughed softly and put his mug down on the table. 'Sorry—getting a bit heavy here. Tell me about your day.'

She studied him thoughtfully for a moment, then smiled, allowing him to change the subject. 'Well—let's just say I've had better. Freddie was a nightmare, Beth decided it was going to be one of those days when she wanted to make things with her mummy and so wanted my un-divided attention, Kizzy was miserable and the decorators wanted tea.'

'Just another peachy day in suburbia, then,' he said with a suppressed smile, and she chuckled.

'Absolutely.'

'So you didn't get a lot of work done.'

'Not so you'd notice.'

He nodded, feeling the prickle of guilt for the umpteenth time that day. 'Sorry. That's my fault. How about I have the kids for you tomorrow so you can rest and do a bit of work and get your head together?'

'That would be fantastic. I've got a roof terrace design to deliver to Georgie and Nick—the one I was working on last night—and if you could bear it, I'd like to take it over to them in the morning and discuss it. It's up to you.'

'That's fine. You do that. I'll cope, I'm sure.'

Except it didn't quite work like that.

Kizzy had other ideas. She woke at eleven, and he fed her, but she didn't seem to want her feed, and then she woke again just after twelve, and he was trying to get her to take the bottle when Em appeared in the kitchen, her eyes tormented.

'Harry?' she said softly.

'She just won't take it.'

'Want me to try?'

He shrugged and handed her the baby and the bottle, but she spat it out and turned to Em, nuzzling her.

And Em turned those tormented eyes on him and said, 'Oh, Harry, I have to…'

She was going to feed her. Again. Bare her breast and put the baby to it, and he was standing there in the kitchen in his boxers and it was all just too much.

He swallowed hard and nodded. 'Sure. Go on up to bed with her and I'll bring you tea,' he said, and the moment she was up there, he ran up, found a long T-shirt and pulled it on to give his emotions a little privacy. Then he went back down, made two mugs of tea and carried them up to her room, putting hers down on the bedside table.

'Call me when you're finished, I'll change her,' he said, and was heading for the door when her quiet voice stopped him.

'Stay and keep me company?'

'Don't you mind?'

She shook her head. 'It's not like it's anything you haven't seen before, is it? The places you go in the world, women do it all the time in public.'

But not her. Not his Em, feeding his child. But she was right, it was nothing he hadn't seen before, and so he sat down on the other side of the bed, propping himself up against the headboard and trying not to stare at the little puckered rosebud lips around her nipple.

'I don't think I've got enough milk for her,' Em said regretfully after a few minutes.

'Is that going to be a problem?'

She shook her head. 'No, not really. I'll be able to give her comfort, if nothing else, and she can get her feeds from you.'

Except she wouldn't. Not then, not later, not in the morning. It seemed she was a baby of discernment, and she'd decided only Emily would do.

Well, she'd made a rod for her own back with that one, Emily thought, and wondered where they went from there.

At best, she was feeding every three hours. At worst, it was more like one and a half or two hours. And, OK, at the moment Harry was living there, but once the decorators had finished and gone and he moved back, was he going to come through the gate in the fence every two or three hours through the night to bring the baby to her to feed?

Or, worse, leave the baby with her?

No way.

She loved Kizzy, wouldn't harm a hair of her fuzzy little head, but she wasn't hers, she hadn't asked for this and there was no way she was taking on responsibility for her. And she was in no doubt that Harry would put up a token fight and then give in and let her if she so much as hinted that she was willing.

She needed an exit strategy and, frankly, until she could convince Kizzy to take the bottle again, she wasn't going to have one. And another thing. How would she explain it to her children? Sure, they'd accept it, but would they then go and tell the world? Kids were so open. OK, not Freddie, although he might be jealous and start wanting to feed again, as well, but Beth might very well say something at playgroup or to Georgie or the boys.

She closed her eyes and stared sightlessly down at the little scrap busy making herself at home with her adopted milk bar. 'Oh, Kizzy,' she murmured. 'Why me?'

But she knew why her. Because nobody else would have been rash enough. They would have let her yell and handed her straight back to her father the minute he walked through the door.

It was her own fault, and she was going to have to deal with the consequences.

Just until she could talk Kizzy out of it. And in the meantime, she was supposed to be going to a business meeting with Georgie and Nick, and how the hell was she going to explain this to them? She'd just have to time it exactly right...

Damn.

Kizzy was yelling again, Freddie wanted to make another sandcastle with a moat and couldn't make the sand pile up because it was too dry, Beth wouldn't help him get water because she was busy pestering Harry for help with putting stickers on a book, and he was ready to rip his hair out.

How on earth would Em cope?

He took a deep breath, thought about it and went into the kitchen, stuck a bottle in the micro-wave—just for a quick blast on low—filled the plastic jug with water and took it to Freddie, helped Beth line up two stickers down the edge of the book and went back and grabbed the bottle.

Slick.

Except she wouldn't take it, Freddie spilt the water and Beth wasn't happy with just two stickers, she wanted more and she wanted him to help her stick them on.

Great. Fantastic. Where the hell was Emily? He glanced at his watch and was stunned. She'd only been gone three quarters of an hour!

'Are you OK? You look really tired.'

She gave Georgie a weak smile and flannelled. 'Harry and the baby are staying with me at the moment, and the baby was up a lot in the night.'

Georgie tipped her head on one side and studied her thoughtfully. Too thoughtfully. 'You've still got a thing for him, haven't you?' she said softly. 'And he's staying with you? Is that wise?'

Not in the least, but she wasn't telling Georgie that!

'It's fine,' she lied, 'but I really ought to get back.'

'Rubbish. He can cope. It does them good—they find hidden strengths. Look at Nick. Fifteen months ago he didn't have a clue about children. Now he's an expert. It's just practice.'

'Well, I don't need him practising on my children,' Emily said firmly, and scooped up her bag and keys. 'Are you sure about the design? Quite happy with it?'

'Absolutely. You've seen the place in London, you know what Nick likes and you've come up with a design that works for him and for the site. What's not to be happy with?'

Emily nodded. 'OK. Great. Thanks. And I

haven't forgotten the bit round the back you want looked at. I will get round to it. It's just that at the moment with Nick's commercial stuff and with Harry and the baby...'

'It's fine. It'll keep. We won't do anything with it till the autumn anyway, so relax. And go back to him, if you have to. I must say if I were you and there was a hunk like that waiting for me, I wouldn't want to hang around having coffee with a chum!'

'But I do,' she said, meaning it. 'I'd love to have time with you, talk to you...' She trailed off, and Georgie's eyes sharpened.

'Em, are you sure everything's OK?'

For a moment she hesitated, wondering whether to say anything, but Georgie probably wouldn't understand. This was her first pregnancy, she'd never fed a baby—she might be horrified. 'I'm sure,' she lied again, and, kissing Georgie's cheek, she bent to touch Maya's head and smile at her, then headed home.

And just in the nick of time.

She could hear Kizzy as she turned onto the drive, and her let-down reflex was working overtime. She squashed her nipples with the heels of her hands and ran into the house, dumped her bag and went out into the garden, to find Freddie yelling and throwing sand out of the sandpit, Beth sulking over her stickers and Harry pacing helplessly with the flailing baby in his arms.

The look of relief on his face was comical.

'You're back,' he said needlessly, and without a word she took Kizzy and the bottle, went down to the seat under the apple tree and tried to fool her. Not easy, with Freddie climbing up her legs and Beth hanging round her neck from behind and Kizzy busy spitting out the teat.

'Hey, kids, how about some juice and biscuits?' she suggested, and looked up at Harry pleadingly.

'Good idea,' he said, picking up on it immediately. 'Come into the kitchen and we'll see what we can find. And you'd better wash your hands first. Come on, young man, let's go and find that biscuit tin,' he added, prising Freddie off her legs and setting him on his feet, then herding him towards the kitchen.

Now, then. She tried again with the bottle, but it was futile, so she hitched up her vest top, unclipped her bra—a front-fastener, dug out of the bottom of her underwear drawer—and plugged the baby in.

Peace. And with any luck she'd get enough food inside her before her children came back out and saw what she was doing. Not that she had any problems with them knowing, it was the rest of the world, and since she didn't intend to let this become a long-term thing—like, more than today, if possible!—there didn't seem any point in them finding out.

All she had to do was convince Kizzy that the bottle was just as good.

She tried sneaking the teat of the bottle in beside her nipple, but Kizzy was smarter than that. She spat it straight out and went back to the real thing.

So much for Plan A.

CHAPTER FIVE

'Houston, we have a problem.'

It was the evening, and she'd spent the day dodging her children every time she'd fed the baby, while he'd struggled to keep them entertained and out of mischief.

Which, to give him credit, he'd managed very well, but it was getting silly, and she'd had a lot of time to think about it.

He cocked an eyebrow at her. 'Want to elaborate?'

'This feeding thing. It's not going to work. Not long term. I shouldn't have started it, it's my own fault, but now I have, I have to find the way out.'

'So what do you suggest?' he asked, his eyes troubled. 'Any ideas?'

'I'm going to see if I can get hold of a breast pump. I've used one before, when I had Freddie, because I had tons of milk and they were desperate in our local special care baby unit.'

He nodded, and she realised he would have known about it from his time there with Kizzy. His next words confirmed it. 'They had one in our SCBU,' he said, smiling crookedly. 'That's where Kizzy's milk came from—they called the thing Daisy. I doubt if you'd get one like that, though.'

'Oh, no, but I'm sure there's one I can get to use at home, but I don't know where from. I'm going to talk to the health visitor in the morning. I know her—she'll sort it if she can. But once your house is decorated, you'll be moving back, and we're going to have a problem if she still wants me. We have to wean her off me, Harry—and fast.'

He was frowning. 'So what's the plan? Give her bottles with your milk in until she gets used to the bottle again, then switch back to formula?'

She nodded. 'That's the idea.'

He pressed his lips together, ran a hand through his hair and nodded agreement. 'Yeah. Well, it makes sense. I can't expect you to do it for ever. Or at all.'

She sensed there was something he wasn't saying, but she didn't push it because she didn't want to be talked out of it. Wouldn't be talked out of it. No matter how sorry she felt for Kizzy.

'Can I borrow your computer and go online?' he asked abruptly.

'Sure.'

She watched him leave the room, and dropped her head back with a sigh. How on earth had she got herself in this mess?

Five minutes later he stuck his head round the door. 'Come and see,' he said, and she got up and followed him to her study.

'Breast pumps,' he said, pointing at the computer with the air of a magician. 'Manual, electric, single, double—tons of stuff. Bras to hold them in place so you can work while you do it—whatever. Order what you want—and get the works. It comes next-day delivery and I'll pay. It's the least I can do.'

The stuff turned up the following afternoon, and she disappeared with it to experiment. He tried not to think about it. He was getting fixated, and it was ridiculous.

'Hey, Freddie, come here, little man. Let's put some more suncream on you and you need that hat on.'

'No!' he screamed, throwing himself over backwards and flailing. 'Not hat! Not cream! Go 'way!'

A window flew open upstairs and Em leant out, clutching a towel to her chest. 'Is he OK?'

'He's fine. He doesn't want sunblock.'

'Bribe him,' she advised, and shut the window.

Huh? Bribe him? A nineteen-month-old baby? With what?

'He likes bananas,' Beth said softly in his ear, and giggled. 'So do I. And biscuits. 'Specially chocolate ones.'

'Is that right?' he said, slinging an arm round her skinny little shoulders and hugging her. 'And I suppose you want one, too?'

'Course,' she said, wriggling free and grabbing his hand. 'C'mon. Freddie, let's get a biscuit.'

'No! Want Mummy!' Freddie yelled, and Beth just shrugged and headed up the path to the kitchen, towing Harry in her wake.

'No biscuit if you don't come. Or banana. Come on, Harry. Let's have a tea party. We'll make some for Mummy, too.'

So he went with her—no choice, really, unless he let go of her hand, which he was curiously reluctant to do—and they made tea and put biscuits and fruit out on plates while he watched Freddie out of the window to make sure he didn't come to any harm.

He'd rolled onto his front, and he was still sobbing, but at least now he was in the shade and he wouldn't come to any harm.

'What's Mummy doing?' Beth asked while she was arranging the biscuits for the fourth time.

'Um—feeding Kizzy, I think,' he said, hoping she wouldn't go upstairs, but she just carried on arranging the biscuits until she was satisfied.

'There. Shall we take them in the garden and wait for Mummy?'

'Good idea,' he said. 'Have you got a picnic blanket?'

Her eyes lit up. 'So we can have a picnic under the tree! Um—Mummy has—it's upstairs, I'll get it,' she said, and before he could stop her, she was gone.

He groaned inwardly, but there was no point going after her and, anyway, he couldn't take his eyes off Freddie that long. Hopefully Emily would have finished by now…

'What are you doing?'

Emily looked up at Beth, standing in the doorway swinging on the doorhandle and watching her, and gave up.

'Kizzy needs milk, but she doesn't like the milk from the shops, and she hasn't got a mummy.'

'So are you giving her your milk?'

'Yes. Like I did when Freddie was small, and I went to the hospital and gave them milk for the tiny babies so they could have it in their bottles.'

'Because Kizzy's tiny, isn't she?'

Emily nodded.

'So why don't you just feed her like Freddie?' she asked, looking puzzled.

Why not, indeed? Except that she wasn't her child, and cradling her that close, suckling her, was going to make it all the harder when Harry took her away.

'Because I can't. Harry needs to move back to his house when it's decorated, and I've got to work. And I don't want to be up all night, I'm tired.'

'Oh. Won't she mind?'

Probably, but it was tough. 'She'll be fine,' she said firmly, hoping it was true. 'Did you come upstairs for anything in particular?'

'Picnic blanket. Harry and me made biscuits and bananas and tea and juice—oh, and strawberries. We're having a picnic in the garden. Are you coming, Mummy?'

Made biscuits? She would have smelt it. Probably just poetic licence. 'In a minute,' she said, eyeing the reservoir and wondering if it would be enough. 'Take the blanket down and I'll be down soon.'

Although not that soon. She filled a bottle, then washed out the machine, put the parts into fresh sterilising solution and right on cue, Kizzy started to cry.

The acid test, she thought, and, scooping the baby up, she offered her the teat, squeezing a little milk out so she knew it wasn't formula, but Kizzy wasn't fooled and she spat the teat out.

Great.

Emily didn't know what she was doing. If only she hadn't started this. Well, it was time it stopped. Harry could feed her. Maybe that would work better.

She took Kizzy down, handed her and the bottle over and gave him a crooked smile.

'Yours, I think,' she said, and, scooping Freddie up, she hugged him and kissed his sticky, chocolaty little face. 'Hello, gorgeous,' she said, and he snuggled into her and wiped chocolate all over her front.

She didn't care. It didn't matter. All that mattered was that Harry and Kizzy would manage to get the milk down her neck and she could take a back seat.

'Is that my tea?' she asked, and Beth nodded.

'It's not very hot.'

'It'll be fine,' she said firmly, and, turning her back on Harry and the baby, she sipped her tea, nibbled a biscuit—not home made, she noticed—and tuned out the sound of Kizzy fussing.

And then, miraculously, there was peace.

The screaming stopped, there was a suckling noise from behind her, and she felt her shoulders drop about a foot.

Finally.

* * *

'Thank you.'

She looked up and smiled at Harry. He was hesitating in the doorway, his eyes studying the gadget, and he shifted awkwardly, jerking his head towards the pump.

'So how does it work?'

Strangely shy suddenly, she showed him the instructions, showed him the bra which held the breast shields in place while the pump was working, and how the milk was collected, and his brows clumped together in a frown.

'I had no idea it was so complicated,' he said. 'Hell, Em, I'm sorry. It's a real drag having to do all that.'

'It's fine,' she said, all too conscious of the fact that he'd never asked her to start this.

'But it's going to take so much time—all the sterilising and stuff, never mind the time linked up to the pump.'

'Well, that's OK. You'll have plenty of opportunity in between milking times to hose down the parlour,' she said with a grin, and his face dropped.

'Me? You want me to wash it out and sterilise it and stuff?'

'Well, why not? She's your baby. I'm just the dairy cow—and, no, you can't call me Daisy,' she added, and his mouth quirked in a smile.

'Sorry. I didn't think. Of course I'll do it. Just one thing?'

'Mmm?'

'Can I call you Buttercup?'

He ducked out of reach, laughing, and she stood up and grabbed a cushion and lobbed it at him just as he turned the corner into the hall.

It bounced off the wall, and she heard the sound of his retreating chuckle, then the noise of the kettle boiling. Two minutes later he was back with a cup of tea for her.

'Kids are all settled. Anything I can do for you?'

A massage, to take the kinks out of her neck from falling asleep in the chair this morning after she'd fed Kizzy?

She shook her head. 'No. I'm fine.'

'You don't look fine, you look tense,' he said, and, turning her round in her swivel chair, he put his big, gentle hands on her shoulders and squeezed. 'Tight as a bowstring,' he said, tutting, and worked the muscles carefully.

Bliss. It was absolute bliss. The only thing that could be better would be if they were lying down, and then when he'd massaged her shoulders, he'd run his hands down her back, over her bottom, her legs, then back up, really slowly, teasing, slipping his finger under the elastic of her knickers and running it round, just enough to torment her. Then he'd roll her on her back and start again, kneading—

'Are you OK?'

Oh, lord, had she really groaned aloud?

'I'm fine. Sorry, bit tight there,' she flannelled, wondering if she'd get away with it. He paused a moment longer, then his fingers started working again and she let her breath go in a long, silent sigh.

'Better?'

Was she imagining it, or was his voice a little husky? No. Don't be silly, she told herself. You're imagining it.

'Yes, thanks,' she said, and wondered if her voice was a little off kilter or if she was just imagining that, too. But then she turned to smile her thanks, and met his unguarded eyes.

Need.

That was what she saw. Need, and hunger, and reluctance. Well, she knew all about that. All of them, in fact. Just at the moment reluctance was way down her list, but it was still there, smothered by the need and hunger and the unrequited ache that had been there for what seemed like half her lifetime.

Was half her lifetime.

Oh, hell.

She turned back to the desk. 'I'd better drink my tea,' she said, a touch unsteadily. 'It'll be cold. Thanks for the massage—I'll be able to put in another couple of hours at the drawing board now.'

She felt him hesitate, then with a murmured, 'See you later, then,' he went out and closed the door softly behind him.

She sagged against the desk and closed her eyes. Why? Why on earth had he had to come back and torment her like this? And why was it all so incredibly complicated?

She straightened up, pulled the file towards her and sorted through the pages, considering the next project she had to do for Nick. She couldn't afford to think about Harry now. She had work to do, to earn her living. And Harry Kavenagh was just a distraction she could do without.

He shouldn't have touched her.

Just the feel of her shoulders, tense under his hands at first, then gradually relaxing, and that little moan—hell, he'd nearly lost it.

Bit tight? Rubbish. She'd been utterly floppy and she'd only tensed up again after she'd made that needy little noise.

And her eyes, when she'd turned—wary,

longing—he had no idea how he'd got out of there. If she hadn't turned away when she had, God knows what would have happened.

He snorted. Well, of course she'd realised that. That was why she'd turned back to her desk, because she'd realised that if she kept looking at him like that, he would have lost it.

Might still.

He growled with frustration and checked his watch. Eight-thirty. He'd fed Kizzy at seven-thirty. With any luck he'd got another hour, at least. He tapped on the study door and opened it a crack.

'Are you OK if I go for a walk? Kizzy should be all right for a bit.'

'Sure,' she said, her voice a little strained. 'Take your mobile.'

'Done,' he said, and went out into the blissful evening. It was gorgeous—a light breeze to take away the heat of the day, the sun low in the sky, creeping down to the horizon. He walked to the clifftop and sat watching the sun brush the sky with colour. It was the wrong way round for a sunset, of course, facing east as it did, but sunrise would be glorious.

If he was up one night, woken by Kizzy, he might bring her here and let her see the dawn.

He glanced at his watch, surprised at how dark it had become, and realised he'd been longer than he'd meant to be. Still, his phone hadn't rung, so Kizzy hadn't woken.

Unless Em just hadn't phoned him.

He jogged back and arrived just as she began to whimper.

'Milk's in the microwave,' Em told him, meeting him in the hall.

'Thanks.' He ran up and lifted the baby into his arms, and she snuggled into him, her little mouth working, feeling the material of his T-shirt and growing impatient.

'Sorry, baby. Do I smell wrong? Never mind. Come on, let's go and find some milk for you.'

Em was waiting for him, handing him the bottle and going back into the study and shutting the door. Just as well. A little space would do them both good at the moment.

He fed the baby, persevering through her fussing until she took the bottle in the end and settled down to suck, then he bathed and changed her and put her to bed.

Ten. Just in time for the news, he thought, and watched it in silence on the edge of his seat, saw friends of his reporting from places he knew well, read between the lines, guessed the things they weren't telling or had been ordered not to report.

Did they miss him? Were they all having to work extra shifts, or were there things not being given coverage because he wasn't there? Maybe some youngster was getting his first chance. Or hers. There were plenty of women now out there working in the field, covering stories every bit as dangerous as the ones he covered.

He laughed softly to himself and shook his head. The most dangerous thing he had to do at the moment was dodge one of Kizzy's special nappies.

Or Emily. Keeping out of her way, keeping the simmering need between them under control because frankly things were complicated enough without that. And then she stuck her head round the door.

'I'm off to bed now. The breast pump's in the sink—it needs washing up and putting in the sterilising solution. There are four bottles in the fridge—should see her through. 'Night.'

'Good night,' he said automatically, and switched off the television. They'd got onto the local news, and he didn't need to know about the local protests about a meat-rendering plant and the woman who'd had her dog stolen.

So he went into the kitchen and picked up the breast pump. Warm. It was still warm, the bits that went over her nipples still holding her body heat, the reservoir warm from the milk.

And he had to wash it, knowing where it had been, aching to have touched her as closely as these bits of plastic.

Dear God, he was losing it. It was just an

ordinary, everyday thing, and he was turning it into something huge.

Because it was.

He didn't know anybody else who would have done it for Kizzy, and it brought a lump to his throat. He didn't want to be there in the kitchen. He wanted to be upstairs with Em, cradling her in his arms, holding her close to his heart, listening as her breathing slowed into sleep, but he didn't have the right.

He didn't have any rights.

He washed it up, put it in the solution, checked the bottles and went upstairs to bed.

Kizzy slept right through to four, and when she woke she snuggled down into his arms and fell asleep again, so he went down to the kitchen, warmed the bottle and went back up, laid her carefully down on the bed and pulled on his jeans and T-shirt, wrapped her in her fleecy blanket and went down, took the bottle and headed for the cliff.

'We should just make the sunrise,' he told her, and as they turned the corner, he saw the first tiny rim of gold creep over the horizon.

'Look, Kizzy,' he said, holding her up, and she opened her eyes and stared up at him and smiled.

She smiled at him! Her first smile!

He sat down on the damp grass, cradled her close and lifted the bottle to her mouth, and she took it without a murmur, while he sat there and watched the new day dawn and marvelled at her smile.

'Harry?'

He turned in the bedroom doorway, his face perturbed. 'Em—I'm sorry, did I disturb you?'

'Not really. I heard the door go. I was worried. Is everything OK?'

He nodded, his face somehow lit from within. 'She smiled at me,' he said in wonder. 'I took her out to watch the dawn and she smiled at me.'

Oh, she remembered that so well—the first time Beth and Freddie had smiled at her. Such a wonderful gift. Of course, Kizzy was very young, so it might have been wind, but she wasn't going to spoil his moment. And she'd been staring more and more intently, so it could easily have been a proper smile.

'That's lovely,' she said softly, and reached out her finger to stroke it down the baby's downy cheek. 'Did she take the feed?'

He nodded, and she felt a strange mixture of emotions. Relief, of course, but also—regret? Really?

'I'm just going to change her and put her down. Do you want me to make you a cup of tea, as you're up?'

She nodded. 'That would be nice. In fact, why don't I make it while you do the baby?' she offered, and he smiled gratefully and went into the bedroom to change her.

Emily went downstairs, put the kettle on and made the tea, and she was just at the foot of the stairs when he came out of the baby's room and pulled the door to.

'Ah, cheers,' he murmured, and ran lightly down, smiling at her.

'So where did you go?' she asked, curious about his sudden urge for the dawn.

'The cliff top. I took the bottle and fed her while I watched the sun come up. It was gorgeous. Beautiful. You would have loved it.'

She would have. Sitting on the cliff top with him, leaning against him and watching for that first sliver of gold—they'd done that on the morning of his grandmother's funeral, and then that night, in the summerhouse, he'd kissed her as he'd never kissed her before, with a wildness and desperation that had nearly pushed them over the edge.

Did he remember? Yes, of course he did. He'd mentioned it already, when he'd talked about the creaking garden gate; she'd said they'd been kids, and he'd said not the last time. So clearly he remembered it.

She handed him his tea and curled up on the chair—safest, really, considering how vulnerable she was to him—and he sat in the corner of the sofa opposite and drank his tea and watched her as the sun slowly pushed back the night and the shadows receded.

'I ought to go back to bed and catch a few more minutes—Freddie'll be up soon,' she said, putting down her mug and standing up, and with a fleeting smile she turned on her heel and left him while she still had the determination to do it.

She was out for the count. Not surprising, really, considering how much sleep she'd lost over the last couple of nights, but as he was up anyway with Kizzy, it was no hardship to give Freddie a hug and change his nappy—quite a different proposition to Kizzy's!—and take him downstairs for his juice.

Two babies, he thought, and had to stifle a slightly hysterical laugh. Him, the greatest bachelor of all time, changing nappies at six-thirty in the morning?

His mother would be stunned.

He realised with something akin to astonishment that he hadn't told them yet—not about Carmen, not about his marriage, and certainly not about Kizzy.

Perhaps he should. Give them an opportunity to gloat. They'd probably earned it, he'd given them a hard enough time when he'd been growing up.

And whose fault was that? an inner voice asked. Yours, for being bored and understimulated by parents that didn't bother, or theirs, for neglecting your basic need for human interaction?

Well, he was getting plenty of human interaction now, both at work and at home—and there was that word again.

'San'castle,' Freddie demanded.

'How about breakfast first?' he suggested evenly. 'Want some eggy bread? Or toast and honey?'

'Eggy b'ed.'

'OK. I tell you what, you drink your juice and watch the telly with me, and I'll give Kizzy her milk, and then we'll have eggy bread. OK?'

''K,' Freddie said round the spout of the feeder cup, and snuggled up under his arm and watched him feed the baby.

He looked exhausted.

He was dozing on the sofa, Kizzy sleeping in the crook of his arm, Freddie next to him watching baby-telly in the crook of his other arm, and Emily felt a wave of emotion that she didn't want to examine too closely for fear of what she'd find.

'Hi, baby,' she said softly, and Freddie lifted his head and gave her his gorgeous beaming smile and held out his arms. She scooped him up, hugged him close and sat down on the chair with him without a word, so as to not disturb Harry. She didn't like leaving Kizzy there like that, in case he rolled over or moved and dropped her, but the first sign of movement and she'd be there.

Plus, of course, it gave her the perfect excuse to study him as he slept.

He was rumpled and tousled and gorgeous, she thought, his jaw dark with stubble, his lashes dark crescents against his cheeks. His nose had been broken at some time, leaving a little bump in the middle, and there was a faint scar slicing through the stubble—from a knife blade? Could be. It wouldn't surprise her, the places he ended up and the trouble he seemed to find.

What was that saying? Don't borrow trouble, it'll find you soon enough—or something like that? It certainly found Harry—or he found it. As a child he'd been a daredevil, and as an adult—well, she couldn't bear to think about the things he'd done in the course of his career as a TV world affairs correspondent.

Still, it was over now. She was sure he'd still travel the world, but once he'd worked his notice, hopefully his life should be a whole lot safer.

And maybe, just maybe, he'd find that life in Yoxburgh wasn't so bad after all...

CHAPTER SIX

'It's looking really good.'

'Mmm.' Harry swivelled round, studying the newly painted sitting room, then glanced down the hall. 'The kitchen's still awful.'

'Well, give them time. I tell you what, if you had the cabinet doors painted while they're in there, it would give it a new lease of life. Just until you decide what you're doing,' she added.

She was fishing, but he didn't rise. 'I'll talk to them,' he said, and disappeared upstairs to where the boss was working, leaving her there with Freddie in her arms and Beth at her side, wrinkling her little button nose at the smell of paint.

Emily was standing by the French doors, keeping an eye on Kizzy outside in the baby-carrier, and she glanced up at the garden, looking at it properly for the first time in ages. As she studied it Harry appeared at her shoulder and made a thoughtful noise.

'Awful, isn't it? It's gone to rack and ruin over the last ten years. My grandparents would be gutted. It just needs tidying when I've got time,' he said, but she laughed.

'I don't think so. Most of the shrubs are too leggy to recover, and it's a high-maintenance garden, anyway. Tenants won't want that, and I don't suppose you do, either.'

'So what do you suggest?'

She shrugged. 'I don't know. Something simple? Some gravel, some paving, some serious pruning and thinning of the shrubbery and some more inventive planting—I'd have to look at it.'

'Would you? I'll pay you to design it for me.'

She turned and frowned at him. 'I wouldn't dream of charging you!' she said, insulted, but he just arched a brow.

'Do you charge Nick?'

'Well—yes, but it's business.'

'Yes. And so's this. Put it like this, if you won't let me pay you, I'll get someone else in—one of the garden centre chains. Most of them have a design department. And you'll have to look at it over the fence and it will annoy the hell out of you.'

'But I'll need someone to look after the children.'

'I'll do that.'

'Only if you let me pay you.' Hah. She had him.

Or not. 'But I still owe you babysitting time,' he pointed out archly, 'and, come to think of it, a massage.'

'You gave me that the other night.'

'Not a proper one. I only did your shoulders.'

And that had been bad enough. The thought of taking her clothes off and lying down on a towel while he massaged her whole body with those incredible hands was enough to make her hyperventilate. She turned back to the garden.

'Fair cop,' she said, her voice a little uneven. 'OK. Instead of the massage, you can look after the kids and I'll do you a design. If you like it, you can pay me. If you don't, then there's no charge.'

'Is that how you normally work?'

'Yes,' she lied.

He grunted, and she guessed he didn't believe her, but it was tough. She wasn't taking money off him if he didn't agree with her design, and she wouldn't take much off him anyway. And she'd oversee it for nothing and pretend it was part of the service. Maybe even do some of the work. And maybe he could do some, too. They could do it together, working side by side while the children played in the soil and ran around getting grubby.

Just like a family.

The sudden ache in her chest took her by surprise, and she sucked in her breath and turned back to him with an overbright smile. 'Deal?'

'Deal,' he said, but before he could say any more or lay down any conditions of his own, her mobile phone rang.

'Hey, Georgie!' she said with relief. 'How are you?'

'Fine—fancy the beach? We're going down with the kids and taking a picnic. Want me to do enough for you, too?'

'You don't want to do that! I can make something for me and the kids.'

'Aren't you forgetting Harry?' Georgie said, and she shot him a look, wondering if he'd heard. Probably.

'Fancy going to the beach with the kids?' she asked him, hoping he'd say no, but he grinned and nodded.

'Love to. I haven't been to an English beach for years. Bucket–and–spade time, eh, Freddie?'

Freddie was jiggling on her hip and squealing, Beth was bouncing on the spot and nearly tugging her arm out of its socket, and Harry looked almost as enthusiastic.

'I think that's a yes,' she said to Georgie, giving up the unequal struggle, because, in fact, she couldn't think of anything she'd like more than going to the beach with Harry and the children.

And if it was just another example of them playing happy families, well, maybe he'd find it was so much fun he wanted to do it again and again and again…

'Freddie, no!'

He was being crushed to death! He was lying flat on his back, buried up to his neck in sand, and Freddie was bouncing on his chest and laughing. Beside him Nick was similarly buried, with Dickon sitting on him and giggling helplessly, and he turned his head and caught Nick's eye.

'Enough?' Nick mouthed, and he nodded.

'OK. One, two, three!' Nick yelled, and they both erupted out of the sand, grabbing the giggling children and dumping them in the dents they'd made.

'Look! I can still see you!' Beth said, pointing at his impression in the sand, Freddie sitting in the middle of it,—giggling hysterically.

''Gain!' he yelled.

'You've got to catch me first,' Harry said, and headed for the sea, Nick at his side and the children in hot pursuit. As his feet hit the water he stopped dead and gasped. 'Hell, it's freezing!'

'Not quite Sharm-el-Sheikh, I'm afraid!' Nick replied with a grin. 'We can always go back to the house for a proper swim if you want.'

'You've got a pool?'

He nodded. 'And a hot tub. I love my hot tub. I've got one in London at the apartment, and I couldn't bear the thought of not having it, so we built one here.'

They strolled along the fringe of surf, the children giggling and chasing each other round and round in the shallow water and splashing each other, while Georgie sat under a big hat and fanned herself and Em sat with her, the baby at her side under a little parasol she'd found in the loft.

They could have been just two normal families, he thought, but of the four of them only Em was really a parent, although of course time would soon change that for Nick and Georgie, with the birth of their own baby in just a very few weeks.

He glanced up the beach at Em. How would he feel if she was pregnant with his child?

Terrifed, if he had any sense.

But apparently not, because the thought didn't seem terrifying at all, it seemed ridiculously appealing—although that was probably because it was never going to happen. One, because he didn't just go round getting women pregnant and, two, because there was no way he was getting that close to Emily.

And if that left him feeling just a little hollow inside, it was tough. Coming back had caused enough havoc. And he needed to be able to leave again, needed to be free—and he knew, just knew, that if he and Em ended up having an affair, free was the last thing he'd be.

'Stay for the evening. We were going to have a barbeque and a real swim, and the children could lie down in front of a film with Nick's mother while we sit outside in the hot tub and chill. What do you say?'

Emily hesitated for a moment, then thought of all the good reasons why not. Starting with the fact that Kizzy was out of milk.

'That isn't really fair on Liz, dumping three extras on her, and anyway, we can't—we didn't bring enough bottles for the baby,' she said truthfully.

'Well—Harry, why don't you go and pick some up from home and come back? We'll look after Kizzy for you, won't we, Em?'

She met his eyes in desperation, hoping he'd catch on, and he did, bless him, but not in the way she'd thought. Instead he grinned and said, 'Sounds like a plan. Except I've had a beer, so I can't drive. Still, you could go, Em. I'm sure there are things you want to do at home—you said something about putting the washing on before you came out, and I don't think you remembered.'

'No—no, I didn't,' she said, grabbing the

lifeline. 'Um—so, I'll go, then, and stick a load in and get everything. Back soon. Kids, be good for Harry, won't you?'

And with a quick kiss for them both, she shot out of the door before Georgie could scupper her by offering to keep her company. The last thing she needed while she plugged herself into Buttercup was an audience!

But she escaped without intervention, and half an hour later she was on her way back, the bottles full and the washing on—just to make it less of a lie, because she hated that. She ought to just tell Georgie and have done with it, but she was afraid her friend would find it somehow repellent.

Still, she'd done her bit for the subterfuge now, and she arrived back armed with the milk and more nappies and clothes for Freddie and Kizzy, to find them all in the swimming pool, with much shrieking and giggling going on, and Nick and Harry with Dickon and Harry junior on their shoulders, battering each other with brightly coloured foam poles.

Dickon fell off with a great shriek, and the two Harrys punched the air and whooped.

'We-e wo-on,' Harry junior chanted, brandishing his hideous green pole overhead and grinning for England.

'Me, me!' Freddie yelled, reaching out to Harry, his little fists opening and closing in appeal, and so Harry took him on his shoulders, Nick took Beth and, as she'd known she would, Beth let her little brother win, falling into the water with a mock cry. Nick scooped her up instantly, hugging her and whispering something to her that made her giggle deliciously, and then she caught sight of Emily and waved.

'Hello, Mummy! Come in the water, it's lovely!'

Why was it, she thought, that the sea was somehow so much less personal, so much easier to be almost naked in? Because here, in the close confines of the Barrons' pool, she felt suddenly hideously conscious of the scantiness of the perfectly normal one-piece swimsuit that only an hour ago had seemed quite adequate.

Not now, though. Now, it could have been made of gauze, and she could feel Harry's eyes burning holes in it

She slid under the water, mmmed appreciatively and swam away from him to Freddie, bobbing happily in his waterwings and splashing Georgie with his pudgy baby hands. He snuggled up to her, giving her a wet, slightly chlorinated kiss, and she was glad to focus her attention on him. It gave her a chance to ignore Harry, although she could hear another loud and boisterous game behind her with him evidently in the thick of it.

'Get the washing sorted?' Georgie asked, and Emily was so, so glad she'd made the effort.

'Yes, thanks. Baby clothes,' she flannelled. 'Kizzy and Freddie. They get through them so fast.'

'So can't Harry use the washing machine?' she murmured, and Emily felt the colour creeping into her cheeks.

'Of course he can—but he didn't know where

Freddie's stuff was. I just popped a few of the baby's things in to make up the load.'

Oh, she was going to be struck by lightning in a minute, and Georgie, who'd known her for years, was giving her a very odd look. She didn't say anything, though, and Nick was getting out of the water and attending to the barbeque, the children were heading for the shower—one mess she was glad she wouldn't have to clear up!—and Freddie was pulling the sort of face that meant she had just a few seconds to get him to a potty.

'Oops. Got to fly,' she said, and hoisted Freddie out of the pool, hauled herself up onto the side, grabbed him and ran.

'That was a great evening.'

She smiled warily. 'Yes, it was.'

'They're lovely people.'

'Yes.'

'You're lucky to have such good friends close by. Mine are scattered all over the world.'

And whose choice was that? she could have said, but she didn't, she bit her tongue and headed for the kitchen. 'Tea or wine?' she asked, and he shrugged.

'Whatever. I've had wine and beer already today. If you're drinking I'll join you, but I'm quite happy with tea.'

'Tea it is, then,' she said, glad she'd had the excuse of driving to refuse the wine, because while she was still expressing milk for Kizzy she didn't want to drink.

And it would be lovely to reach a point where she didn't have to take that into account at every moment of her life!

With a little sigh she put the kettle on, reached for the mugs and bumped into Harry.

'Sorry,' he said, throwing her an apologetic smile. 'I was getting the mugs for you.'

But the damage was done. After a day of watching him running around on the beach and at the Barrons' three parts naked, water sluicing off his powerful body and beading like tiny gems in the dark hair that covered his legs and arrowed down his abdomen, just the brush of his body against her was enough to start a wildfire that no amount of common sense was going to be able to put out. She'd nearly blown a fuse when his leg had brushed against hers in the hot tub, but she'd been safe there, with Georgie and Nick to chaperone and keep order. Here, there was no one to hold them back, nothing to stop them. Except her fleeting common sense.

Emily turned back to the tea, her fingers trembling, and dropped a teaspoon on the floor.

They bent together, bumped again and he laughed and apologised and moved away, giving her room to breathe at last and her heart time to slow.

'So—fancy having a look at the garden tomorrow?' he said after a long moment that sizzled with tension.

'Sure. If you have the kids.'

'I thought we could do it together—talk it

through. It's not as if it's far away. The kids can come, too. After all, it's the weekend. The painters won't be there.'

'No. OK. What did they say about the kitchen, by the way?' she asked, desperately trying not to think about that arrowing hair on his washboard abdomen.

'Oh, he'd been going to suggest it,' he said, taking his mug from her. 'Thought it was a good idea for a short-term fix. He's going to do it.'

'Colour?'

Harry shrugged and grinned. 'I have no idea. Maybe sort of duck-egg, I think he was suggesting, but I can't say I've taken an interest in kitchens, really. My flat's got a stainless-steel and lacquer-red high-gloss laminate kitchen that's a mass of fingermarks and a living nightmare to work in—not my choice, I have to add. It was the developer who put it in. The only bit of it I like is the walnut worktop, because it goes with the floor. Anyway, it doesn't matter. This kitchen can't look worse than it does at the moment, so duck-egg or cream or whatever, it has to be an improvement.'

They went through to the sitting room and she picked up the TV remote. 'Want to watch something, or shall I put music on?'

'Music would be nice,' he said, and she went into her study and came back with a couple of CDs that she used for background while she was working—compilation albums of soft, easy-listening tracks, female singers mostly, but she'd never noticed just how intrinsically romantic all the songs were until that moment.

Damn. She should have chosen something different—something classical. She buried her nose in her mug and tried not to look at him. For a few minutes they sat in silence, then the third track came on, less romantic, and with an inward sigh of relief she shifted slightly so she could see him better and said, 'Tell me about yourself. What have you been doing since I last saw you? Apart from the obvious, of course.'

He gave a quiet huff of laughter. 'Nothing

much. Flying about all over the world. It doesn't leave time for much, really.'

'You'd just left uni when your grandmother died, hadn't you? You must have been twenty-one, I suppose.'

He nodded. 'Nearly twenty-two. And you were nineteen, and home from uni for the summer.'

And they'd watched the sun rise, and then that night…

The memory was written on his face, and she looked away. 'So what did you do then? After you left?'

He shrugged. 'Bummed around. Took the gap year I'd never had, saw some of the world, worked in a radio station in Brisbane, got a job on a newspaper in Rio, linked up with a television crew in Nepal, and that was it, really. I started doing odd bits for them, earning a living but nothing great, working as a news researcher when I came home. Did a bit of local television news, then got the break into overseas reporting when I was about twenty-five. I've been doing it for six years now.'

'And you've never married?'

He shook his head. 'Well, except for Carmen, and she didn't really count, because I'd realised by then that I'd never marry. It just doesn't fit with the job.'

'You're not telling me all those reporters are single?'

He laughed. 'No, of course not, but they find it hard to have a normal family life. I didn't want anything in the way. And anyway, I'd never met anyone who made me feel like settling down.' He tipped his head on one side. 'So tell me about you. I know about Pete but what did you do before you met him? How old were you then?'

'Twenty-four. I'd finished my degree, decided biology didn't really qualify me for anything and, anyway, I'd discovered I loved gardens, and so I did a garden design course and started work.'

'Here.'

She laughed. 'Well, yes, my father let me do their garden, and I did some others, and then I worked for one of the garden centre chains—

the sort of thing you were threatening me with yesterday.'

He grinned. 'Hardly threatening.'

'Blackmailing, then. Anyway, that's what I was doing when I met Pete.'

'And you stopped when you had Beth?'

'Only for a while,' she told him, remembering her reluctance to go back to work full time. 'I wanted to freelance, to break out on my own and work from home, but he said we couldn't afford the risk. What he really meant was that he wasn't prepared to fund me while it got off the ground, but Pete never really said what he meant—not until he walked out, and even then he didn't discuss it.'

Harry shook his head. 'I can't believe he just legged it while you were at the supermarket.'

'Pausing only to stop the credit card,' she reminded him. 'Still, water under the bridge and all that. And I'm much happier now than I was then.' Except for the fact that she couldn't afford to house her children without her parents' generosity. That was a bit of a killer, always nagging at the back of her mind.

As if he'd read that mind, he said quietly, 'And the house? I don't imagine if you weren't living here your parents would want to keep something this big on into their retirement.'

She shook her head. 'No. Ideally they want to downsize and buy somewhere in Portugal, as well, to be near my grandparents. Well, my mother does. My father would be quite happy here, pottering in his garden, but he loves her, and whither thou goest and all that.'

He frowned. 'I can't imagine a woman in the world who'd want to follow me wherever I go.'

Or a woman, presumably, who he'd follow?

'To the ends of the earth,' she murmured, realising that, were things different, if she hadn't had the children and if he'd asked her, she would follow him anywhere he asked her.

'It sometimes feels like it,' he replied. 'And, like I say, no sane woman would want that.'

No sane woman, possibly, but where Harry

was concerned she could never be accused of being sane. If she was sane, she wouldn't have ended up sharing her roof with him, making him welcome, feeding his child for heaven's sake!

'So how's Dan?'

Dan? 'He's fine,' she said, reining in her rambling mind and concentrating on her brother. 'He's working in New York. He breezes in from time to time, sometimes without warning—he's got a partner, Kate, but there's no sign of them getting married, to my mother's disappointment. She wants to see her firstborn settled, she says, before she turns up her toes.'

His eyes narrowed. 'Is she sick?' he asked, and she laughed.

'No, not at all. She's just despairing of Daniel. No, she and Dad are fine. Enjoying life.' And she was holding them back, interfering with their plans for retirement. Oh, damn.

'Em, are you OK?'

She met his eyes, gentle and concerned, and

could have crumpled, but she didn't. 'Yes, I'm fine,' she said. 'Just a bit tired.'

'Why don't you turn in?' he suggested.

She gave a wry smile. 'Another appointment with Buttercup before I can go to bed, but I've got half an hour or so to kill, at the least. I might go and sort out the washing and tidy the kitchen.'

But the kitchen was tidy, and the washing could wait for the morning so she could put it on the line, so she just pulled it out of the machine into the plastic basket ready for the morning. She'd stick it by the door and then she wouldn't forget, she thought, but he was in there with her, right behind her again, so that when she straightened up and stepped back with the washing basket in her hands, she cannoned into him and felt her head connect with his chin.

'Ouch!'

'Oh, Harry, I'm sorry!' she said, turning to see if she'd hurt him, and found him ruefully rubbing his jaw, the fingertips rasping over the stubble and sending shivers skittering over her nerve endings.

He took the laundry basket out of her hands and put it down again. 'I think it needs a magic kiss,' he murmured. 'Like the ones you give Beth and Freddie when they hurt themselves.'

'Big baby,' she teased. She must be mad. She shouldn't rise to it, he was just being silly. She hadn't really hurt him. Still, she lifted his fingers away, went up on tiptoe and pressed her lips to the spot, just because it was so irresistible.

'There. Magic kiss, all better now,' she said softly. And just as softly he replied, 'You missed. It was here,' and, turning his head, he touched his lips to hers.

For a moment her heart lodged in her throat, but then it broke free, beating wildly against her ribs, deafening her with the clamour of its rhythm. Deafening her to reason, certainly, because instead of moving away, taking herself out of reach, she went back up on tiptoe, slid her arms around his neck and kissed him right back.

He groaned softly, easing her closer, and she felt his fingers thread through her hair and cup her head, anchoring it against the onslaught of his mouth. Then the kiss gentled, and he lifted his head a fraction, dropping a daisy chain of hot, open-mouthed kisses over her cheek, her eye, down the side of her jaw. He traced a line around her ear, his breath teasing her hair and making it stand on end, then he moved on, down the side of her neck, across her throat, pausing over the wild fluttering pulse before continuing down, down, across her collar-bone, her shoulder, the slope of her breast.

He lifted his head and stared down at her. 'You've caught the sun,' he murmured, one finger trailing over the sensitive skin of her cleavage. 'Do you have any idea,' he went on gruffly, 'just what you've been doing to me all day, running about in that little scrap of black Lycra?'

He traced the line the costume had followed, down, up—back down again...

She sucked in a breath and her ribs lifted, bringing his knuckles into contact with her breast, and he groaned again, his hands sliding down to bracket her waist, easing her closer as he trailed his tongue over the sun-warmed skin, leaving fire and ice in its wake. With a muttered oath he lifted her vest top out of the way, unclipped her bra and tenderly, reverently, cradled the burgeoning fullness of her breasts in his hard, hot hands.

He sucked in a breath, his head lifting so he could stare down at her, and his pupils were huge, his eyes dark as midnight with desire. His thumbs dragged over her nipples, sending sensation arrowing through her and bringing a cry to her lips, and slowly he lifted his hand and stared at it.

There was a bead of moisture on his thumb, pearly white, and as she watched he lowered his head and touched his tongue to it.

His eyes were still locked on hers, smouldering with unspoken need, but the touch of his hands had triggered her natural response, and she felt the milk beading on her nipples.

'Harry, no,' she moaned, anguished, and

lifting her hands to his shoulders, she pushed him away, her heart clamouring, her body aching for him but common sense, finally, making itself heard.

And he dropped his hands and stepped back, swallowing convulsively, and turning on his heel he strode away, up the stairs and into his room, closing the door softly but emphatically behind him.

With a whimper Emily crumpled against the worktop, her hands trembling too much to deal with the breast pump for a moment. And so she stood there, her legs like jelly, until her breathing had slowed and the world had righted itself and her hands were hers again.

Then she gathered all the bits and pieces from the steriliser, went into her study and shut the door every bit as firmly. Two doors between them was the minimum they needed at the moment.

She sat down, set up the equipment and reached for her CD player to relax her—and then remembered that her favourite, most relaxing CDs were in the sitting room.

And she'd never be able to listen to them again without thinking of him.

Five more nights, she told herself. That was all it was. Five more nights until he was back in his own home and she had her house back to herself.

It couldn't come a moment too soon.

CHAPTER SEVEN

'THAT'S a bit more like it!'

Em stood back and studied Harry's work, and nodded. 'You'll get there. Take the cut down another notch and run over it again. You never know, you might even find a lawn in there!'

And she turned back to her surveying, measuring, checking sight lines and jotting notes on a pad. Busy. Busy, busy, busy since the sun had crept over the horizon and he'd been dragged out of bed by Kizzy's first whimpering cry. She'd been up minutes later, going downstairs while he'd fed Kizzy and tried so hard not to think about last night.

The feel of her. The taste.

The look of longing in her eyes before she'd

pushed him away and stepped back, bringing their unscheduled and very unwise kiss to an end in the nick of time.

More or less. His dreams had been colourful, to say the least, and he'd been glad to get up just to get away from them.

Then while he had been changing Kizzy's nappy and looking out of the window, she'd taken the washing down the garden and hung it out in her nightshirt and bare feet, standing in the dewy grass and stretching up to the washing line so that her nightshirt rose up and gave him the occasional glimpse of her smooth, firm bottom encased in its sensible white knickers.

Since when had sensible white knickers been such a turn-on?

Not that he'd been looking, of course. Just glancing down the garden while he'd changed the baby's nappy and put the kettle on to make them tea and loaded the washing machine with his clothes and emptied the dishwasher—

anything that just happened to give him a view out of one of the back windows!

Then she'd come back in, stood with one foot rested on the other like a child, staring at the floor for a moment until she'd lifted her head, sucked in a breath and said, 'About last night.'

And without giving her a chance to get in first, he'd said, 'I know. I'm sorry. It was stupid of me. It won't happen again.'

And she'd stood there, opened her mouth again, shut it, and then finally said, 'Good. Right. So. About your garden.'

And that was that.

No more talk of the kiss. They'd shut the door on it, walked away and now they were laying waste to the jungle that had been his grandparents' pride and joy.

'Right. That looks better. OK, I've done the survey. I just want to walk you through these shrubs and agree which ones should come out and which ones we can prune and rescue.'

'Is August the time to prune?'

She shook her head. 'No, not really. It's too hot. We need to wait a bit, but we can trim them. There are rules, for spring and summer flowering shrubs, for roses, for evergreens. But I think when you're talking this drastic, you just have to do what you have to do and hope they make it through. Most of them do. Right. Let's make some decisions and mark them up.'

And she picked up a can of yellow spray paint and headed down the garden, relentless.

Ten minutes later and the yellow kiss of death was on many of the bushes. 'Your job, I think. I'll put them through the shredder and keep an eye on the children. Beth, put that down, darling, it's sharp. Freddie, no!'

She took the secateurs from Beth, the dirty stick from Freddie before he put it in his mouth again, and handed Harry some very businesslike pruners. 'Get to it, then.'

He lifted a brow, tugged his forelock and set about the mammoth task of flattening the garden.

* * *

She really didn't need this.

She was sitting in the shade with the children, Freddie napping on her lap, the baby asleep in the carrier beside her, Beth sitting cross-legged playing a game with stones and talking happily to herself, and in front of her Harry was stripped to the waist and digging.

Rippling muscle, smoothly tanned skin glistening with sweat, streaks of dirt across his forehead where he kept lifting his arm and wiping away the trickles that threatened to run down into his eyes. And the way he threw the spade down into the hole, over and over, slicing through the roots and then grasping the stem and heaving it over, trying again, cutting another root, another tug, another cut, and all the time those muscles bunching and gleaming and driving her crazy.

Finally, victorious, he heaved the rootball of a huge old viburnum out of the ground and straightened, grinning at her. 'At last,' he said, his breath sawing in and out, and he strolled over, dropped down beside them and reached for a glass of fresh lemonade.

'Oh, bliss,' he said, rolling it over his chest and then lifting it to his lips, his throat working as he swallowed it in one.

'I hope you never go to wine-tastings,' she said drily, and he chuckled.

'Oh, I can swill and spit with the best of them, but ice-cold real lemonade on a hot day with a raging thirst? No way. It would be a sin to spit it out.'

'Want another?'

He grinned. 'I thought you'd never ask.'

He held out the glass while she filled it from the Thermos flask, then took a long, reflective swallow and smiled. 'Gorgeous. Nice and sharp. I hate it too sweet.'

'It's got honey in it,' she told him.

'It's lovely. Thank you.'

She dragged her eyes away from him, from those twinkling, smiling eyes, the stubbled jaw—she hadn't given him time to shave she'd been in such a hurry to keep moving—the beads of sweat caught in that fascinating, arrowing hair just above his battered old jeans…

No!

'Want to have a look at the plan? It's only a doodle so far—nothing formal yet—but I'd like your feedback.'

'Sure.'

And he lifted the tray out of the way, set it down on the other side of him and shuffled closer.

Too close. She could smell him, the tang of fresh sweat, the warmth of his skin, the lemons on his breath—intoxicating. She hauled her pad over and picked up a pencil.

'I thought this might work,' she said, and forced herself to concentrate.

It took two days.

Two days in which Harry thought his muscles were going to die, but it was only because he'd been too busy with the baby to work out. Normally, in his crazy nomadic lifestyle, he stayed in hotels that had gyms—unless they were filming in the back of beyond, in which case very often they'd had a hike to get there—and when he was at home in London he went to the gym round the corner from his flat.

But in the two—or was it nearly three?—weeks since Kizzy had come into his life, he hadn't lifted anything heavier than a basket of wet washing, and he needed this.

Therapy, he told himself, and at least he'd slept last night.

And now, at the end of the second day, the shrubs with the yellow squirt on them had been evicted, a rotten tree was felled and the root hacked down to below ground level, and a huge pile of shredded material was heaped up at the bottom of the garden ready to be composted and put back into the soil. He tipped out the last bag onto the heap with a sigh of relief and surveyed the devastated garden thoughtfully.

'It looks vast,' he told her. 'I'd forgotten the garden was so big.'

'They always look like this when they're cleared. Even cutting the grass can double the apparent size of a garden. And using fine lawn grass does the same thing, because we have a mental scale rule and a blade of grass is x big, therefore the garden must be y long—and so on.'

'Tricks of the trade? Clever. So what's next?'

'Marking out the hard landscaping, deciding on the shape of the lawn, and then getting down to the nitty-gritty of the planting. But to do that, we need a big rope to lay on the ground to give us a line. There's one in the summerhouse. Can you give me a hand? It's quite heavy.'

The summerhouse?

'Sure,' he said, his mouth suddenly dry. He hadn't been in the summerhouse since the night of his grandmother's funeral. He'd been actively avoiding it, because so much of their past was in the place, but it seemed his avoidance tactics were to come to nothing.

Right now.

He followed her, Freddie and Beth running

ahead to show him the way, Kizzy sleeping in the carrier in the shade by the back door where they could keep an eye on her from either garden.

And there it was, screened by shrubs, tucked away at the end in a lovely, private little dell, the sort of place that as children had been a magical retreat, and as adolescents in the grip of their hormones had been an ideal trysting place.

'Right, it's in here somewhere,' she said, pulling the door open and picking her way in. 'We don't use it any more, so it's a bit of a dumping ground now. Ah, here it is.'

It smelled the same. Slightly musty, the odd cobweb hanging across the windows, and it had gone downhill a little, but it was basically the same, and the memories slammed through him.

The hedgehog with its fleas. Secret societies with Dan, and Emily and Georgie, on occasions, if the girls insisted. And then later, on her sixteenth birthday, their first kiss.

Tender, tentative, staggering in its impact on the seventeen-year-old boy with a massive chip on his shoulder and a feeling that he'd never really been wanted.

Until then.

But Emily had wanted him, and, God help him, he'd wanted her. So much.

That innocent, simple kiss had awoken a whole world of sensation that had somehow been much more than straightforward lust. It had been the tenderness that had shaken him. Her tenderness, and his. Particularly his. Until the night of his grandmother's funeral. That hadn't been tender. That had been desperate, and frightening, and wild with a passion that had left them both shaken. They'd stopped, pulled back from the brink, shocked by the force of their emotion—

'Harry?'

He lifted his head and met her eyes, and the memories must have been written all over his face. 'Sorry. Miles away,' he said, and he watched the soft colour sweep her cheeks and she looked away.

'Um—the rope,' she said, but she was between him and it, and the only way to get it was to squeeze past her. She turned away from him, but as she struggled not to fall headlong into the piles of clutter, he took her shoulders in his hands to steady her and her bottom settled briefly but firmly against his groin.

She gasped softly and squirmed past him and away, out of the door, and he sucked in a huge breath, forced himself to concentrate and reached for the rope. If she had any sense, she'd tie him up with it and leave him there to cool down.

'Uncle Dan! Mummy, look, it's Uncle Dan!'

'Hi, Half-Pint. Hello, little sister—got room for a lodger for a few days?'

Dan's voice came to him through the open door, and Harry took a moment longer to steady himself while Emily ran to greet him.

Then he followed her out of the door and hesitated on the step, the rope in his hands. 'Might be a small problem with that. I seem to have borrowed your bed,' he said, stepping forward out of the doorway, and Dan did a mild double-take.

'Harry?'

He felt the smile start, right in the centre of his chest, along with that strange tightness and the prickling in his eyes. 'Well, hi, stranger.'

'Me, stranger? Coming from you?'

He laughed and—typical Dan—crossed the garden in two strides and engulfed Harry in a hug. 'Ah, hell, you're all sweaty! Since when did you get your hands dirty?' He laughed, and let him go.

'Since your sister started cracking the whip,' Harry replied with a wry smile. 'God, it's good to see you again. You are the world's lousiest communicator. How are you?'

'I'm the world's worst? And you're so darned good at it?' he returned, but Harry noticed he hadn't actually answered the question, and the smile on his face didn't really reach his eyes.

'So what's going on? What brings you back?' he asked, but Dan just shook his head.

'Never mind me, what brings you here?'
And right on cue, Kizzy started to cry.

It was hours later, and the children were in bed.
Dan's luggage was installed in their parents'
bedroom, because, as Emily had pointed out,
Harry was about to go back to his own house and
it would be silly to change the beds just for two
or three nights. They'd had supper and were
sitting down with a glass of wine and catching up.

Well, she wasn't drinking, and any minute
now she'd have to sneak off and deal with
Buttercup, but if Daniel was going to be staying
there—and he still hadn't said why he was there,
or how long for, or where Kate was—he was
going to find out sooner or later.

Later, preferably.

'I feel nibbly—jet-lag,' he said, and got up
and went out to the kitchen, coming back a few
moments later with another bottle of wine and
a party-sized packet of hand-fried potato crisps.
He ripped them open, tipped them onto the table

and sat down, propping his feet up just inches from the crisps.

'So where's Kate?' Emily asked him, fed up with waiting for him to say anything and going for the direct approach. 'Kicked you out because of your disgusting habits?'

He gave a laugh that sounded just a little hollow to her ears, and reached for some crisps. 'Never mind about Kate, what's all the gubbins in the sterilising solution? Looks like bits of a breast pump. Don't tell me Freddie *still* isn't weaned!'

She shot Harry a desperate look, and he just shrugged.

OK. So she was on her own here.

'It's for Kizzy,' she said, being deliberately evasive. 'She doesn't tolerate formula very well.' OK, slight exaggeration, she'd been fine with it until she'd realised there was a choice, but he didn't have to know that.

He stared at her thoughtfully, then turned to Harry and said, 'So tell me again how this happened? You just found some kid on the street and *married* her? Bet that caused a wave of grief through your little black book.'

Harry's jaw tightened. 'I don't have a little black book,' he replied, and Dan snorted.

'Last time I saw you, you were fighting them off with a stick—and not trying too hard, if I remember correctly.'

'I was young.'

'Oh, and you're so ancient now, poor old man. All of—what are you, six months older than me? That makes you thirty-one, right? Almost thirty-two? And you married a total stranger because you felt *sorry* for her? Man, you are nuts. And now you're living here with Emily and she's feeding your baby? And I thought I'd just pop home for a few quiet days!'

Emily gave him a strained, apologetic smile. 'Sorry. Of course, if you'd rung…'

She left it hanging, and he shrugged and reached for another handful of crisps and another glass of wine. 'Last-minute flight,' he said lightly, and she realised he still hadn't said anything about Kate.

Well, they all had something they didn't want to talk about. And she had no doubt he'd tell her in the end. He always had, but she just had to wait and bide her time. In the meantime, he was still grilling Harry.

'So what did your boss say when you dumped this on him?' he asked.

'Her. And you don't want to know,' Harry muttered. 'Let's just say it wasn't pretty.'

Dan threw back his head and laughed. 'I'll bet. So that's it? No more crazily dangerous reporting from Harry Kavenagh in Timbuctoo?'

'It's still up in the air,' he said evasively. 'I've got a month.'

'Three weeks,' Emily put in. Not that she was counting. And she didn't dare ask what the outcome of his deliberations would be, because she was hoping against hope that he'd pack it all in and stay there and things would…

Dan was letting his breath out on a long, low whistle. 'That's a tough one. It all backfired a bit on you, didn't it? I mean, if you just married her to give her a better life, you didn't intend presumably to be a father? I mean, not a real one. Not this real, at least. So what the hell are you going to do?'

Harry reached for the crisps and sat back casually. 'We'll see,' he said, but there was nothing casual about the tic in his jaw or the way his free hand was crushing the crisps to dust, one by one in the palm of his other hand.

And for the first time in years, Emily realised she wasn't actually pleased to see her brother, because his arrival would interfere with the dynamics between her and Harry, and the cosy little family unit she was trying to create felt suddenly very threatened…

'So what's the real story, our kid?'

Dan spoke softly, standing beside her and propping up the worktop, long arms folded across his chest, hazel eyes searching.

'Real story?'

'Harry. Why's he back here?'

She shrugged, not sure she knew the answer. 'He just turned up one day with the baby. He'd been sent home from the hospital with her, and didn't know what to do. He came here.'

'The only place he's ever called home,' Dan said quietly.

She met his eyes.

'And you?'

He looked away. 'Just needed space.'

'From Kate?'

'All of it.'

'Business not going well?'

He shrugged. 'Business is fine. I'm just not sure of my direction at the moment. Did Nick Barron tell you I ran into him in New York a few weeks ago?'

'He did mention it. Said you were in good form.'

He chuckled. 'It was the end of a long party. George had the baby yet?'

'No—four more weeks, I think. We spent Friday on the beach with them. She's looking good—coping well.'

'Unlike Harry.'

'Oh, Harry's doing fine. It was a bit of a steep learning curve, but he's great with her now and he's wonderful with Freddie and Beth. Beth adores him.'

'Isn't that dangerous?'

She nodded, biting her lip. 'She knows he's just a friend—that he's going again. I've told her.'

'And you? Have you told yourself, little Em?' he said softly.

'Endlessly.'

'And do you believe it?'

She shrugged away from the worktop. 'I have to, don't I? Because one of these days Harry Kavenagh's going to pack up his bags and go, and I have to be ready for that.'

'And Kizzy?'

She stopped, her heart aching. 'I have no idea what he's planning for Kizzy. It's none of my business, and I'm keeping it that way.'

'If you say so,' he murmured.

'I do,' she said firmly, and headed for the stairs.

'Sis?'

She turned back to him, reluctantly because she knew all she felt would be written on her face, and he gave a quiet sigh and shook his head. 'I thought you would have got over him after all this time.'

'I have,' she said, her voice even firmer than before, and turning on her heel, she walked resolutely away.

Behind her, Daniel shook his head.

'Oh, Harry, what have you done?' he said under his breath, and went to find his old friend.

'So what really brings you back to Suffolk? Em tells me you aren't a frequent visitor.'

'More frequent than you,' Dan replied, but Harry wasn't having that.

'We aren't talking about me, we're talking about you,' he said. 'And I get the distinct feeling that you rocking up here out of the blue is rather more meaningful than you're letting on.'

'I could say the same for you—and since my

sister seems to be very much at the heart of this situation, I would very much like to know why.'

'Why what?' he asked wearily. 'Why I came back here? They told me to take my baby home. This came to mind. It seemed like a good idea at the time.'

'And now?'

Harry met his eyes, then looked away, giving his hands an unreasonable amount of attention. 'I'm not here to hurt her, Dan. We're just friends. She's helping me out of a jam—offering me and Kizzy a roof over our heads while the decorators are in and until the new furniture arrives. Nothing else.'

'Except she's feeding your baby.'

Harry felt his neck heat and ran his hand round it, letting out a harsh sigh. 'That wasn't meant to happen. Kizzy wouldn't take the bottle. I was in London for the day, she didn't know what else to do.'

'So she got out the breast pump and fed her?'

He prevaricated for a second, then said, 'Something like that.'

Dan's eyes narrowed. 'Hell! She breastfed her, didn't she? Damn, I might have known. She's as soft as lights, that girl.'

'She's a woman, Dan.'

'Oh, I've noticed—and I might have known you had. Things were never the same after the summer she turned sixteen. I would have thought you'd both moved on from a teenage crush, but perhaps I've been naïve.'

Harry stabbed his hands through his hair and growled softly under his breath.

'Dan, me and Em—there's nothing to it. She's just an old friend.'

'So you haven't touched her, then? I mean, I know you're in my room, but that might just be for the sake of the children. A cover story.'

He jackknifed out of the sofa and strode across to the window, glowering down the garden. 'That's just fantasy.'

'Yours?'

Bastard. He felt the colour rise on the back of his neck, the guilt plucking at him.

'So have you touched her?'

'I really think that whether he's touched me or not is none of your damned business, Daniel,' Em said from the doorway, and Harry swore softly and turned to face her.

'Em, don't chew him out, he's only doing what he's always done.'

'Yeah—interfered! Well, it isn't necessary, Dan, so give it a rest. We aren't kids any longer. I'm going to bed. I suggest you two do the same and maybe by the morning you will have got some common sense.'

And she stalked off, leaving them both suitably reprimanded.

'Bossy little madam.'

Harry turned and gave Dan a thoughtful look. 'Fancy a drop of Irish whiskey?'

'What—for old times' sake?' He grinned wryly and got to his feet, slinging an arm round Harry's shoulder and slapping it affectionately. 'Why not? Got a secret stash?'

'No, but your father always did.'

Dan chuckled. 'I believe he still has. Come on, let's raid it. It won't be the first time.'

And maybe, Harry thought, if he softens up enough, he'll tell me what's really going on.

'So what time did you get to bed last night?'

'God, you sound like my mother,' Harry groaned, and scrubbed a hand over his already rumpled hair.

'I thought your mother had no idea what time you went to bed because she was there as little as possible? And maybe I have a flicker of sympathy for her,' she said unkindly.

'Ouch.' He winced and sat down on the arm of the sofa. 'And don't waste your sympathy on her. She didn't know, didn't care—didn't want to have anything to do with me. Let me rephrase that. You sound as if you could be my mother.'

She smiled and relented a little. 'So—what time? I feel I have the right to ask, since this is the second feed I've given your daughter since you crashed into your bedroom at three-thirty this morning.'

'So why ask if you know what time?' he groaned, getting up and heading for the kitchen. 'Tea?'

'Thanks, that would be lovely.'

Kizzy—like Harry and Dan—had finished the bottle, so Emily lifted her up against her shoulder and followed him through to the kitchen.

'So did you get anything out of my brother last night?'

He shook his head. 'Nothing that made any sense, but I have to say I think Kate's at the bottom of it.'

'Mmm. I agree. Oh, rats. I did so hope he was settled this time. They seemed to get on well enough.'

Harry looked at her closely. 'Do you like her?'

Oh, blast. Now she was going to be torn between loyalty and truth.

'That's a no, then.'

'I didn't say a word.'

'No. And you don't hang back for nothing. So you don't like her—or you don't think she's right for him.'

'it's not for me to decide that,' she protested, but her heart wasn't in it. She didn't like Kate— never had, never would. She thought she was superficial and self-serving, and she'd never been able to understand what Dan saw in her. But she'd thought he loved her, was happy with her, and so she'd been happy for him.

She sighed and took her tea, then put it down again, took his from him and handed him the baby. 'Yours, I think,' she said. Picking up her tea again, she went back upstairs to bed. Five minutes, she thought. Just five minutes alone, with a cup of tea and a good book—

'Mummy!'

She gave Freddie a tired smile, scooped him up in one arm and carried him back to bed with her. 'Hello, little man. How are you today?'

''K,' he said cheerfully. 'Want tea!' And he

slid off the bed and headed for the stairs, turning as he got to the top to look back at her.

She saw it coming. Saw the inevitable, but as if her feet were stuck in treacle, she just couldn't get there in time.

'Freddie, careful!' she said, running towards him, but he laughed and turned and then went, in slow motion, end over end over end until he hit the floor at the bottom and was still. She screamed and flew down the stairs after him, arriving a fraction after Harry.

'Don't touch him!'

His voice checked her, but he held her back, then let her go once he was sure it had registered, but of course it had. She couldn't move him in case of making his injuries worse—oh, dear God, what if he'd broken his neck? What if he'd got a head injury?

'Mummy,' he wailed, and, rolling over, he stumbled into her arms, sobbing pitifully.

She clung to him, tears pouring down her face, rocking him gently. 'It's all right, baby, it's all right. You're OK, Freddie, I've got you,' she murmured, over and over again, soothing him until his sobs slowed to a steady hiccup.

She became aware of Dan sitting on the bottom step with his arm around her, Harry crouching beyond her, one hand gently, rhythmically stroking her knee. Beth was standing wide-eyed beside him, a look of terror on her face.

She tried to smile. 'He's OK. I think he's probably just bruised. Freddie, let me look at you,' she said, shocked at how shaky her voice was.

'Head,' Freddie said, rubbing his forehead tearfully. She could see a blue bump coming up, and all her fears about head injuries came to the fore again. 'Magic kiss!' he demanded, and she closed her eyes and pressed her lips, oh, so gently to the little bump.

'There,' she said, her voice shaking still. 'Magic kiss—all better now.'

And then she looked up and caught Harry's eyes, and saw the tenderness and concern for her son in them—and the memory of their own magic kiss in his wry, gentle smile.

'Want tea,' Freddie said, but Harry shook his head.

'He ought to be nil by mouth until he's checked over.'

'Shouldn't I just watch him? Keep him awake and check him?' Just the thought of hours in A and E was enough to make her want to weep, but she knew he was right. 'OK,' she sighed, before he could answer. 'I'll get dressed. Freddie, stay with Harry and Uncle Dan and Beth, and I'll get ready, then we'll go in the car to the hospital and you can see the nice doctors again—OK?'

'Again?'

She looked up at Harry. 'Oh, yes. Freddie lives life in the fast lane. We're regulars. And while I'm gone, could you two find the stairgate and put it up, and give Beth her breakfast, and then, if Kizzy's all right, why don't you both go over to the garden and get started on clearing the patio slabs? But for now a clean nappy on him would be good.'

And handing Freddie over to his uncle, she got to her feet and ran upstairs, her legs like jelly. And shutting her bedroom door, she leant back against it, buried her head in her hands and sobbed.

He couldn't bear it.

'You OK here?' he said to Dan, and he nodded, so Harry went past him and up the stairs three at a time, knocked on Emily's door and pushed it open gently, moving her out of the way and then folding her firmly against his chest.

'Hey, come on, it's all right. He's going to be OK.'

'Not necessarily,' she sniffed, 'and what if he isn't? I took the stairgate down because he was climbing over it, but he just wasn't paying attention. If it had been there, it would have slowed him down. I would have been with him—'

'Shh. It's OK. It's not your fault, it's just life.

Stuff happens, Em. Don't beat yourself up. Come on, let's see you smile.' And he tipped up her head and smoothed the tears from her cheeks. Her mouth wobbled, but to give her credit she drew herself up and smiled.

And he couldn't help himself.

He bent his head, brushed her lips with his and drew her back into his arms. 'There. Magic kiss. All better now,' he said gruffly, and then forced himself to let her go.

'You'd better get dressed and get off. Want one of us to come with you?'

She shook her head. 'I'll be fine. Can you cope without me? I might be hours,' she said unevenly.

'Sure. You go ahead. And don't worry. Beth will be fine. You just concentrate on Freddie, and let us know if they want to keep him in or anything.'

She nodded. 'Will do.'

He went back out, closing the door carefully behind him, and found Dan struggling with Freddie's nappy.

'Want a hand?'

Dan grunted and stood back. 'He's all yours,' he said with a grin. 'How is she?'

'OK. Bit shaken up.'

She wasn't alone. Just hearing her scream and seeing Freddie tumbling end over end like that down the stairs was enough to make his blood run cold.

If anything had happened to the little lad…

Damn. He was getting in too deep. So deep.

Right in over his head.

He had to get the hell out of there and back to his own house before it was too late, he thought, and ignored the little voice that told him it already was—far, far too late…

CHAPTER EIGHT

FREDDIE was fine.

After three hours in A and E of being poked and prodded and X-rayed, they sent her home with him, armed with a head injuries card listing all the things she should keep an eye out for.

He was in fine form. He'd had a good time in A and E, he'd got a sticker on his hand and he'd had lots of cuddles and new toys to play with—life, as far as Freddie was concerned, was great.

Not so for his mother.

She was exhausted, she needed the breast pump fast, Harry's garden was in chaos and all she could think about was going to sleep. She turned into the drive, cut the engine and sat there, eyes shut, wondering if she could find the energy to deal with the day.

It was all Harry's fault, she thought unreasonably. Him and Dan, between them, had kept her awake half the night, and Kizzy had kept her awake the other half. She couldn't do it any more.

'Em? How is he?'

'He's fine. Harry, I can't do it any more,' she whispered. 'Feeding her, being up in the night— I just can't do it. I'm so tired. I've got so much work to do for Nick, and I know we spent the weekend in your garden, but I really ought to be getting on with Nick's stuff today, but I can't because your garden is utterly destroyed and the kids need me and Kizzy needs me and I just can't do it all—'

'Shh,' he murmured, drawing her into his arms and rocking her gently. 'You go to bed. Dan and I will look after the kids and sort out the garden. You have a sleep, and we'll worry about the rest later—OK?'

'But you don't know what to do—'

'Rubbish. We're not stupid. I'm sure we can read your plan well enough to do the basic groundwork.'

'And watch the children?'

'And watch the children. Stop worrying. And I'm sorry we kept you awake.'

'I need to see Buttercup,' she told him, and he frowned.

'I've been thinking—we ought to try her back on the formula,' he said. 'This can't be helping.'

'I still need Buttercup.'

He gave her a fleeting smile. 'OK. Come on, let's get you both in and sort you out. Want a cup of tea?'

'Want tea!' Freddie chimed in. 'And biscuit.'

'He needs breakfast, he must be starving.'

'So do you. Come on.'

And he led her inside, sent her into the study with Buttercup and tapped on the door a few minutes later. 'Room service,' he murmured, and she opened the door a crack and stuck her head round it.

'Tea and toast,' he said, and handed them to her one at a time so she could take them from behind the door. Breastfeeding was one thing. Being connected to the pump was quite another, and she felt ridiculously shy and self-conscious.

She thanked him and shut the door, sat down again at her desk and while Buttercup did her job, Emily looked through Nick's file and studied the brief for her next contract.

It was mercifully simple, but it needed to be stunning and she didn't have it in her to be stunning at the moment. She rested her head on the desk, closed her eyes and sighed. 'Just a few minutes,' she murmured to herself. 'Then I'll do it…'

She'd been ages. He couldn't believe how long she'd been in there, and he could hear the pump still running.

'Em?'

He tapped on the door and opened it a crack, then said her name again, but there was no reply, so he stuck his head round the door and saw her slumped forward on her arms, fast asleep.

'Em?' he murmured, stroking her shoulder gently, and she woke with a start and sat up, her arms flying up to cover her breasts, cheeks burning.

'Sorry,' she said. 'Um…'

'I'll go,' he said, sensing her discomfort at his presence, and he went out and shut the door, resting his head back against it with a sigh.

It was crazy. She was worn out, and helping him with Kizzy wasn't doing her any good at all.

Behind his back he heard the door opening, and he straightened and turned, to find her there with all the pump's paraphernalia in her hands. 'Oh,' she said, and he held out his hands and she put the stuff into them, her cheeks still flushed.

That could have been with sleep, of course, but maybe it was just because she was shy. And he'd pushed her into something she wasn't comfortable with.

She touched his hand. 'Harry, don't look like that, it was my idea to feed her.'

'Well, it's time it stopped. I'll get her back on formula—mix them, perhaps. And the decorators will be done tomorrow, and the carpets come on Wednesday, and the furniture's due then as well. And we'll move out, and you won't have us underfoot or keeping you awake all night any more, and you'll be able to get on with your life. Now, go to bed and get some sleep.'

And he turned on his heel and walked into the kitchen, leaving her there with a lost and mournful expression on her face.

'Fine,' she said softly, and, turning round, she went upstairs to bed.

Kizzy was having none of it.

The best-laid plans and all that, he thought wearily, and went back to the fridge for the real McCoy.

He was exhausted. He'd spent the day in the garden with Dan, lifting the slabs on the patio and breaking up the concrete path that led to it, and in the middle of that he had been keeping an eye on the children, getting them food and drinks, watching Freddie like a hawk for signs of head injury and feeding Kizzy in between.

Only she had other ideas, the little madam, and if he hadn't loved her so much he would have throttled her.

'Problems?' Dan said, dropping down beside him on the grass in the shade and watching him try again.

'She likes Emily milk. Only Emily milk.'

Dan frowned. 'So what's going to happen when you go back to work? Are you leaving her here with Em?'

'I can't.'

'So you'll take her away with you?'

He let his breath out on a sharp sigh and shot Dan a troubled glance. 'I can't do that, either.'

'Rock and a hard place come to mind,' Dan said mildly, lying back on the grass. 'So what, then? You need to do something. I mean, she's not a puppy. You can't just stick her in kennels every time you race off to the other side of the world.'

He felt sick.

For the rest of the day, all he'd been able to hear had been Dan's voice, those words echoing in his head.

She's not a puppy. You can't just stick her in kennels.

So what the hell was he supposed to do?

Especially now she was so inextricably linked to Emily.

He'd begun to realise that every time he got some formula into her, it upset her little tummy. Clearly her system couldn't tolerate cows' milk.

The next day he went to the doctor's surgery and saw the health visitor and explained the situation, leaving Emily's name out of it.

'Oh, this must be Emily's little one,' she said with a smile. 'She's been on the phone, asking for advice.'

He felt silly. 'Oh,' he said. 'So what did you say?'

'Try all the things you've been trying,' she told him. 'Only if she's got a problem with cows' milk, then you've got to try soya milk or carry on as you are. Personally I think breast milk is best, obviously, because it's designed for human babies, and in cases of lactose intolerance like Kizzy's, your choices are strictly limited.'

'Tell me about it,' he muttered, and she smiled and patted his hand.

'It doesn't last for ever. This is only a short phase of her life. Once she's weaned it all gets much easier.'

Really? With him on the other side of the world? He didn't think so.

She's not a puppy. You can't just stick her in kennels.

He thanked her and left, bought some soya milk and tried that. It was better, but she still didn't like it, and when he tried her back on Emily's milk exclusively, she settled straight away.

And his decorators were finished, the carpet fitters were in and the furniture was stacked up on the drive, waiting. He didn't have the time or the energy for any more experiments, and Kizzy was beginning to distrust the bottle.

He found Dan in the swing seat under the old apple tree, reading a book. 'Dan, they've finished in the sitting room. Could you give me a hand to get the suite in?'

He grinned. 'As an alternative to lying here, doing nothing? It'll be a pleasure.'

'Don't be sarcastic. You need the exercise.'

'Exercise?' he grumbled. 'I've been doing nothing but exercise since I got here,' he pointed out.

'I'll bring you a beer under the tree when we've finished,' he promised, and Dan chuckled.

'You must think I'm really cheap.'

'I know you're really cheap,' he replied, and headed for the drive of his house, Dan trailing behind and grumbling. They found Emily in there with the children, Beth picking up the little bits of carpet that the fitter had missed, Freddie making piles of tufts in the middle, and Emily vacuuming up the rest.

She finished the last bit and turned off the machine. 'You'd better give me Kizzy,' she said, and he took the sling off and handed her over reluctantly.

Strange, how odd it felt without her on his front. He'd got so used to the sling he didn't even think about it now, but obviously he couldn't carry her and move furniture any more than he'd been able to do the gardening with her on his front.

And he missed her.

'Right, let's get this suite in,' he said, and didn't let himself think about how he'd feel when he'd gone back to work and left her behind.

You can't just stick her in kennels.

It looked good.

They'd worked all day, following the fitters round, cleaning up each room in turn and unpacking the furniture, and now it was done. Beth and Freddie had been wonderful, but the novelty was definitely wearing off, and the fridge was low on milk.

And Kizzy was starting to grizzle.

So Emily went to pump, and Harry took the last bottle of milk and went to feed the baby, and she sat in her study linked up to Buttercup and thought, How stupid. What a pointless exercise, when she could just be giving it to Kizzy direct.

It wasn't as fresh, there was an infection risk, there was infinitely more work—crazy.

But necessary, for her peace of mind, for Kizzy's independence from her and for the future.

Whatever that might hold.

Emily realised that she had no idea. Dan had told her that Harry was still undecided about what he was going to do, and she had to have answers. She had to know what the future held, she couldn't go on like this indefinitely.

She'd have to tackle him—but how?

And that night he'd be sleeping in his house again.

It felt so odd, not being at Emily's.

It smelt strange—that new-carpet smell, a brand-new bed, the sheets stiff and creased from the packets, the down duvet not yet quite fluffed up.

Not that he really needed it. It was still hot at night, and he lay with the windows wide open and stared through the uncurtained window at the house next door.

Emily.

She was all he could think about.

The landing light was on, the trees filtering the light, but he could still see it.

Kizzy was asleep in the room next door. She'd been unsettled, but that might be because it smelt different. But finally she'd gone to sleep, her tiny mouth working rhythmically, and he'd been able to get his head down.

But just like his daughter, sleep eluded him for a while. Not that he wasn't tired. He was. He was exhausted. Days in the garden, today spent heaving furniture around—all on top of weeks of broken sleep, starting after a hectic fortnight dodging mortars and sniper fire—it was no wonder he was shattered.

But it wasn't enough to stop his mind working.

He went down to the kitchen—a soft ivory, in the end—and made himself a cup of tea. He didn't have anything else apart from coffee in the empty kitchen, and he really didn't need that. And he sat in his sitting room overlooking the now orderly but barren garden, pale in the moonlight, and wondered what the hell he was supposed to do about Kizzy.

'So have you decided what you're going to do?'

He didn't pretend not to understand. He was sitting in the garden with Emily, more than a week after he'd moved back to his house, less than two weeks of his month's grace left, and he still hadn't made a decision about where he went from there.

He shrugged. 'I don't know. I can't see the way forward. I need a nanny, I suppose, but I can't bear the thought of leaving her with a stranger. I just don't know what else I can do, though. I can hardly drag her with me if I get sent to a war zone or a hurricane or an earthquake.'

'You didn't really think this through, did you?'

He looked at her. 'Think what through?'

'Bringing up a baby.'

He frowned, remembering the rain-lashed night when Carmen had been mugged, the night he'd landed and been greeted by horizontal rain and the news that his wife was on life support.

'Of course I didn't think it through,' he said savagely. 'I didn't have time. I'd adjusted to the idea that I was going to be a father, but that was all. Not the implications. Not this. But she was my wife—for better, for worse and all that crap. What was I supposed to do, Emily? Tell them to throw the switch? Let the baby die, just because she was going to be a bit of an inconvenience?'

Em blanched and shook her head. 'No, of course not.'

'No. And you're right, at the time I just didn't think it through. So now we have to deal with it. Correction. *I* have to deal with it.'

'Except it seems to be involving me.'

'Yes. I'm sorry. Well, I've tried. She'll take soya milk. Perhaps we should just give her that from now on, cut you out of the equation.'

'That doesn't help you.'

'It gives me more choices.'

'Of child care?' She shook her head. 'Maybe you should look at your job,' she offered softly, and he stared at her in astonishment.

'My job? I can't change my job.'

'Why not?'

He was shocked. 'Because it's me. It's what I am.'

'No, Harry, it's what you *do*.'

He thought about it for a second. Barely. 'Isn't

that the same thing? Aren't you a garden designer?'

'No. I'm a mother, and I'm me, and I design gardens for people to earn a living. And I'm lucky that I enjoy it. But it isn't me. It's not what I *am*.'

He stared at her for a long, puzzled moment, then reached for his tea, retreating behind it while he thought over her words. Do something else? He couldn't imagine doing anything else. Nothing. The noise, the drama, the terror and pain, the injustice—bringing all that into people's homes and showing them what was going on in the world was how he spent his life.

It was what he *was*.

'I *have* to do it,' he said urgently. 'I have to show people what's happening out there.'

'No. Someone has to, Harry—but it doesn't have to be you.'

'Yes—yes, it does, Em. It does have to be me. It *is* me.'

'In which case perhaps you'd better think about whether you're the right person to be bringing Kizzy up, because if you go back to work and leave her with a succession of un-supervised nannies, then you're no better than your parents, and frankly, you'd all be better off if you gave the baby up for adoption,' she said quietly, and, picking up her tea, she went back inside without another word.

He stared after her, stunned.

Adoption? *Adoption*?

He looked down at the baby on his lap, her head lolling in sleep, and felt a wave of emotion so powerful it nearly unravelled him.

But maybe she was right. Maybe he wasn't the ideal parent for this beautiful little girl. He'd never meant to be her father, not in this way. He'd meant to pay her way, secure her future, make sure Carmen had everything she needed for a good life. A safe life.

And she'd died, as a result of his interference.

Hot tears scalded his eyes, and he scrubbed them away angrily. No. He wouldn't wallow in self-pity. This wasn't about him, it was about

Carmen, and her daughter, little Carmen Grace—the tiny Mini-Dot who'd stolen his heart.

And he owed it to her to do this right.

If he could only know what that was—but he was beginning to wonder if Emily hadn't already told him…

'Seen Harry?'

Emily shook her head. 'Not for ages. Um—I might have upset him.'

Dan tipped his head on one side and studied her thoughtfully, and she swivelled her chair round from the drawing board and recapped their conversation.

'You told him to put her up for adoption? Ouch. I thought *I'd* been harsh.'

'What did you do?'

'Oh, it was days ago. I told him she wasn't a puppy and he couldn't just stick her in kennels every time went off after a news story.'

'Ow. What did he say?'

'Not a lot. He was talking about nannies.'

'Mmm. He was talking about them today, as well, but I don't think he's considered things like time off and shift patterns. He'll need a fleet of them. I don't suppose he's even thought about it.'

'No, he's good at that. Fancy a coffee?'

'No. I've just had one. Now, go away and amuse yourself. I've got work to do.'

'Actually, I was looking for Harry for a reason. I was thinking I might go up to London for a few days. I was wondering about his flat—thought if it was empty, I might scab it off him as a base.'

She felt a rush of relief, followed by guilt, because she still didn't know what he was doing over here from New York and yet all she wanted was time alone with Harry—time in which to change his mind, to convince him that there was more to life than running away from it. And she'd got less than two weeks left.

'I don't think there's anyone in the flat at the moment. You'll have to ask him. Phone his mobile, he's usually got it with him. Is Beth OK?'

'She's fine. She's colouring in the kitchen while I read the paper.'

'Send her in to me if you go out.'

'Will do.'

She heard the door close, and looked down at the drawing in front of her.

Rubbish. It was rubbish, the planting totally wrong. And she couldn't for the life of her work out what was right.

Seemed to be a lot of that going on at the moment, one way or another, she thought, and pushed back her chair. She could hear Freddie stirring from his sleep, the thump of his cot as he turned over and sat up, followed by a little wail. She went up to his room and was greeted by outstretched arms and a watery smile, and she lifted him out and cuddled him close and wondered what on earth she'd do without him.

'Want to go for a walk?' she asked, and he nodded.

'Beach,' he said.

'Maybe. Let's find Beth and ring Georgie. If

they're busy we can go the other way and feed the ducks—'

'Want beach! Want Harry!' he said, his voice rising, and she soothed him and changed his nappy and took him downstairs past the reinstated stair gate.

'Beach!' he told Beth cheerfully. 'San'castle. Mummy, down!'

She put him down and he ran to the door, beaming up at her. 'Harry,' he demanded, but she wasn't at all sure Harry would want to come.

'We'll see. I think he's gone for a walk.'

'With Kizzy?' Beth asked.

'Probably.'

They went without him, taking the buggy in case Freddie's legs got tired, and met him on the cliff top. He was sitting with Kizzy in his arms, staring out to sea, and as Beth and Freddie ran over to him, he lifted his head and looked across at her, and for a fleeting moment his face was bleak.

Then a shutter seemed to come down, and he smiled at the children. 'Hi, kids,' he said, and his voice sounded rusty and unused. 'Going to the beach?'

'The buckets and spades are a bit of a give-away,' Emily said with a laugh, but it cracked in the middle and he shot her a glance.

'Come with us,' she said softly. 'I've brought your shorts—you left them drying in the bathroom. And I brought bottles and stuff for Kizzy. I had a feeling you might be here.'

'Did you come looking for me, Emily?'

His voice was a little hard, and she looked away. 'I'm sorry. I shouldn't have said what I did. I know it's difficult.'

'You have no idea,' he murmured, and got to his feet, tucking Kizzy back in the sling. 'Come on, then, kids. Let's go and build sandcastles.'

They buried him again.

Buried him and jumped on him, while Em sat with Kizzy and laughed and told them to be gentle, and then Georgie came down with Harry and Dickon and Maya, and they ended up back at the Barrons' house, having juice and biscuits and playing in the swimming pool.

And Kizzy ran out of milk.

'Sorry, guys, time to go, we have to feed the baby,' he said, and helped Em dry the children and walk them reluctantly home.

'I wanted to stay,' Beth said mournfully. 'I like Dickon. He's my friend. Freddie's a baby.'

She wasn't much more than a baby herself, he thought, smiling indulgently and hugging her slim shoulders as they walked along.

'There'll be other days. Maybe you can see them again tomorrow or the next day.'

'Tomorrow,' she said decisively, and ran to her mother. 'Can we see them tomorrow?'

'We'll see,' she said, and Beth pouted.

'That means no,' she explained to Harry. 'But I want to see them.'

'Well, we can't always have what we want,' he said, his heart aching, because this little family outing was getting to him, reaching parts of him that had been dormant all his life, and the process, like letting blood back into a limb that had gone to sleep, was a mass of alien sensations. And not all of them were pleasant.

She was sitting in the study, wrestling with the plans for Nick's contract, when she heard the back door open and shut.

'Em?'

She stood up, stretching out the kinks, and went into the kitchen to see Harry there with Kizzy in his arms, his face troubled.

'What's up?' she asked.

He swallowed, looked down at Kizzy and pressed his lips together. 'I've had a phone call from my boss. There's been an earthquake.' He hesitated, then said, 'She wants me to go.'

'But you've got another twelve days!'

'I know. But she wants me now. It's not for long, just three or four days, but...' He shrugged, and she felt a cold, sinking feeling in the pit of her stomach.

'Are you going?'

'I have to.'

'And Kizzy?'

He frowned. 'I wanted to ask you if you'd look after her. I wouldn't have asked, but she hasn't given me any notice. And I know I haven't sorted out any child care, but I'll do it the minute I get back.'

She ignored that. She was too busy thinking about him going to an earthquake zone. Not that he hadn't done it before, but that somehow had been more remote. Now, after these weeks, it all seemed much closer to home.

'So, will you? Look after her?'

'This time,' she said, trying to inject some muscle into her voice, but it didn't sound convincing. 'When do you go?'

'In the morning. Early.'

Just like that, her dream was turning to dust. She felt her eyes fill, and turned away.

'Is Dan here?'

'Yes, he's watching a movie.'

'Tell him goodbye from me. I'll bring her round in the morning, just before I go.'

She nodded, and he turned and went out, all the spirit drained from him.

Why? Why go, she wanted to ask him, but she couldn't. She knew why he was going— because he'd convinced himself it was who he was. Even though he clearly didn't even want to go this time.

She snorted, shut the door and stuck her head round the sitting-room door. 'I'm off to bed.'

'Was that Harry?'

She nodded, but couldn't say any more. 'I'll see you in the morning,' she said, and went upstairs.

She took a shower, so the sound of running water would drown out her sobs, and then she went to bed. Not that she slept, and at four-thirty, when she heard Harry's front door open and shut, she tiptoed into Beth's room and watched him walking down the road, Kizzy in the sling on his front.

She pulled on her clothes and ran lightly down-stairs, slipped out of the door and followed him.

She knew where he was going, and she followed him to the cliff top and sat beside him on the wet grass and tucked her arm in his, her head on his shoulder as he fed Kizzy and watched the sun come up.

Finally he took a deep breath, let it out on a sigh and stood up, helping her to her feet. They walked back in silence, and when they reached her house, he turned and looked down at her without a word.

And still without a word, she took his hand and led him, not down her drive but down his, and in through the door, and up to the bedroom he'd used as a child.

He put Kizzy down, still sleeping, in her cot, and came back to her, his expression guarded, but a muscle jumped in his jaw.

'Are you sure, Em?' he murmured.

She nodded, blinking away the tears.

'Yes.'

And with a ragged sigh, he drew her into his arms.

CHAPTER NINE

'HERE—my house keys. Get Dan to take the cot over later. I meant to do it when I got back from my walk, but I got a little sidetracked.'

His mouth twisted into a sad, fleeting smile, and he drew her back into his arms, his voice muffled by her hair. 'I'm sorry. I hate dumping her on you. I know it isn't fair, but it won't happen again. I've been thinking about what you said, and I've decided you're right. I'll sort all the details out when I get back, but I'm going to put her up for adoption.'

She lifted her head, unable to stifle a little cry, and took in the bleak, empty look in his eyes. 'Oh, Harry,' she said, but there was nothing she could add. There was nothing to say and, anyway, her throat wouldn't work properly, so she just lifted her hands and cradled his face and kissed him.

'Take care,' she pleaded.

He nodded. 'I'll see you soon.'

He kissed her again, urgently, hungrily, and then broke the kiss abruptly, turned on his heel and strode to his car, driving off without a backward glance. She lifted her hand to her lips, her fingers replacing his lips, holding in the anguish.

'Oh, dear God, take care of him,' she whispered, and picking up Kizzy in her little carrier, she went round the side of her house and in through the kitchen door.

Dan was sitting there, Freddie in his high chair having juice and toast, Beth kneeling on a chair arranging her toast soldiers into neat rows and talking to them, and as she walked in with Kizzy Dan took one look at her, stood up and ushered her straight into the hall.

'He's gone,' she said tonelessly. 'His boss

rang last night. There's been an earthquake somewhere.'

'Indonesia. I know. It was on the news. I wondered if they'd call him in.'

She nodded. 'He was there earlier this year, and they want him there again. He knows it well, apparently. It makes sense, but…'

Dan searched her face, then dragged her into his arms and hugged her. 'So what about Kizzy? Are you looking after her until he's back?'

'Yes, but…' She felt the sob beginning to rise and swallowed it down. 'He said I was right. He's going to put her up for adoption. Oh, Dan, what on earth have I done?'

She looked up at him, expecting condemnation, but this was Dan. He just shrugged. 'Helped him organise his priorities?'

'And Kizzy? What about Kizzy?' She swallowed again and stared down at the sleeping baby in her carrier, then answered her own question. 'I guess she'll end up somewhere with a couple who are desperate for a baby. And they'll love her to bits—'

She broke off, and Dan sighed and rubbed her arms comfortingly. 'She'll be fine, Em.'

'But she might not be. What if they split up? What if she ends up in the middle of a divorce?'

'She'll be brought up by a single parent. It hasn't done Beth and Freddie any harm.'

She frowned. 'But—what if she doesn't have the infrastructure I've got? The family and friends, giving support?'

He gave a bemused laugh and shook his head. 'You're making a hell of a lot of assumptions here. They might be fantastic parents.'

But she wouldn't see her again. Ever.

She shook her head and turned away. 'I'm going to put her down in the study and get some breakfast. Thank you for looking after the kids.'

'Any time. But next time you might let me know you're going.'

'There won't be a next time,' she said firmly, and went into the study, put the baby down and then caught sight of the television through the sitting-room doorway. They were showing scenes of the earthquake, and she sat down, hands knotted together, and watched it.

It was dreadful. Scene after scene of devastation. She felt gutted for them, but more than ever afraid for Harry. What if there was another one? There often was.

She was aware of Dan coming up behind her, placing a hand on her shoulder, watching it with her. 'I've made you fresh tea,' he said.

'Thanks.'

'Come on, he's not there yet. He won't be there for hours.'

He was right. He'd said it was a twelve-hour flight, and then he had to get in and out of the airports. It would be tomorrow morning before he appeared on TV. She turned off the television, went through to the kitchen and gave the kids a hug. Freddie gave her one of his special sticky kisses, and Beth snuggled up beside her while she ate her breakfast, mechanically spooning in the cereal without even tasting it.

And he hadn't even left the country yet!

Nick phoned at eleven, when she'd just put Freddie down for a nap and she was working on his plan, Beth at her side colouring.

'Hi,' he said, sounding exhausted and yet euphoric. 'Just had to let you know—Georgie's had a little girl—three point seven kilos, or eight-three in old money, and they're both doing really well.' He hesitated. 'We've called her Lucie, after my sister.'

'Oh, Nick, that's lovely!' she said, her eyes filling. 'When's she coming home?'

'This afternoon. She's absolutely fine, and I'm around and so are my mother and her father, so I'm going to pick her up around three.'

She felt herself welling up. 'Give her my love, and tell her I'll come and see her tomorrow some time, the minute I can get away.'

'You running out on me again?' Dan said,

lolling in the doorway behind her. 'It's a good job I haven't gone to London yet.'

She smiled at him as she cradled the phone. 'Georgie and Nick have had a little girl. I'm not going far. I thought I'd drop in and see her in the morning. If you don't mind looking after the kids?'

He smiled. 'Of course I don't mind. We could walk down and they could play with the others for a few minutes, and then maybe we could go on the beach.'

Except she'd be tortured by images of Harry—Harry buried up to the neck in sand, Harry running into the sea, Harry skimming pebbles with the children, showing off, Harry—just Harry, everywhere she looked.

'Sounds lovely,' she said, just for Beth. 'That would be nice, wouldn't it?'

'Can I hold the baby?'

'Not tomorrow, probably. She'll be too tiny.'

'Kizzy's tiny,' she pointed out truthfully. 'And I hold her.'

'We'll see,' she said automatically, and Beth pouted.

'You mean no.'

'No, I mean I'll see what Georgie has to say about it. It's her baby, after all, and Dickon and Harry will want to hold her. That's a lot of holding for a tiny baby. Right, how about a drink and a biscuit to celebrate?'

Harry wasn't on the ten-o'clock news, but he was on the satellite news at midnight.

He must have scarcely landed, and he was flying by helicopter to the epicenter of the earthquake, jammed in amongst aid workers.

'This is the only way to get here,' he was saying, shouting over the noise of the aircraft, 'because the roads are rubble. They've only just cleared them after the last quake, and now the people of this devastated region are facing destruction and ruin yet again. Down below us everything is flattened, as far as the eye can see. Trees are down, rivers have altered course yet again and every village is showing more signs of destruction. I'm going back to the small community I stayed in last time, to see just how much damage has been done, but early reports aren't good. This is Harry Kavenagh, reporting to you from somewhere over Indonesia.'

The report went to cover other areas, showing more pictures of the damage, but Emily had seen enough. She'd seen him, in his element, back where he belonged.

Being him.

Her eyes pricked with tears, and she blinked hard and turned off the television with an angry stab at the remote.

Dan flicked her a glance, opened his mouth and shut it again. 'Tea?' he said eventually, and she nodded.

'Thanks.'

But she couldn't drink it. She just felt sick, because she'd lost him, and they were on opposite sides of the world.

'I'm going to feed Kizzy and get to bed,' she

said, and went to the fridge. One last bottle after this. She contemplated Buttercup, but frankly she was too tired. She'd do it later, when she'd fed Kizzy.

But she didn't. She was exhausted, struggling to stay awake long enough to feed and change her, and then when she fell into bed she slept so soundly she didn't wake for hours.

Kizzy was starting to cry, and Dan and her children were still asleep, so she crept downstairs, got the bottle out of the fridge and put it in the microwave to heat. She flicked on the television, and there Harry was again, on the early breakfast news, describing the damage sustained by the little town.

She heard the microwave ping and, still watching the screen through the open doors, she went into the kitchen and took out the bottle, but as she turned back, her watch caught on the door and the bottle spun out of her hand and shattered on the floor.

She stared at it blankly. How could it shatter?

They were unbreakable—unless it had already been cracked? She didn't know. All she knew was that the fridge was empty and Kizzy was crying in earnest now.

Forgetting the television, she turned to the steriliser and realised, to her dismay, that she hadn't put Buttercup's bits and pieces in there. They were lying in the sink, rinsed but not nearly sterile enough to use.

And Kizzy was crying, and her nipples were prickling, and the utter futility of it struck her like a brick.

What on earth was she doing? Why on earth express the milk, decant it from the pump into a bottle, then give it to Kizzy?

Especially if she was going to lose her so very, very soon.

With a sigh of gentle resignation, she went back into the sitting room, picked the baby up and sat down with her.

'Look, Kizzy,' she said softly, lifting her night-shirt out of the way. 'Daddy's on the telly.'

And while she watched him, hanging on his every word, his tiny daughter snuggled into her, latched on and fed, contented at last.

'You're crazy.'

'Dan, I had no choice. I broke the last bottle and the things weren't sterilized.'

He smiled and shook his head. 'I didn't mean that. I meant you're crazy trying the pump in the first place when you should have been doing this all along.'

'I was trying to keep some distance,' she explained, and he laughed softly.

'You? I don't think so. I think you're doing what you should have been doing all along— and I think you think so, too.'

She looked down at Kizzy, so dear to her, and swallowed. 'Except when she goes to her new home, it's just going to be even harder for her.'

'Well, I guess there's only one thing for it.'

'What?'

'You'll just have to adopt her yourself.'

She stared at him, aghast, and then turned back to Kizzy, blinking away the sudden tears.

'Don't be silly,' she said, her throat clogged. 'I can't do that. I've already got Beth and Freddie.'

'So what's one more? And you can't tell me you don't love her. I've seen you with her. Look at you—made for each other. How can you let her go?'

She couldn't—and it was going to tear her apart. She looked up at Dan in anguish. 'What part of no don't you understand? I can't do it. I can't afford another child. Especially not this one.'

'Because she isn't really Harry's?'

She shook her head. 'No. Because she is, in every way that matters. And—'

She broke off, and Dan finished the sentence for her. 'And because you love him?'

She looked away. 'I'm so silly. I didn't mean to do it. I didn't mean to let myself get so involved.'

'So why go to him in the night?' he murmured.

'We watched the sun come up,' she said, remembering. 'And because it was in the east, I realised that he'd see it hours before me, and if I go and watch it come up, it'll be over him, getting low in the sky, but he'll still be able to see it.' She looked at Dan and smiled sadly. 'I couldn't let him go again. Not without knowing. I could lose him, Dan. He might be killed. Maybe not this time, but the next, or the next. Maybe when he's reporting on a war. They get shot, taken hostage, murdered, blown up—it happens regularly. And there could be another earthquake where he is now. It's terribly dangerous, everything he does. And I thought, if he dies, and I've never found out what it would be like with him, never held him, never shared that…'

She broke off, not knowing how to say it, but she didn't need to. Dan was beside her, holding her, offering her a tissue and giving her a gentle hug. 'I understand. I would feel the same. And I guess he did, too.'

'It was sort of goodbye,' she said unevenly. 'And maybe—perhaps there was a part of me that hoped it might bring him back to me. Bring him to his senses. Make him realise all the things here waiting for him at home.'

'Maybe this tour will. Maybe it's just what he needs—to go from this to that.'

She shook her head. 'It'll just remind him of what it's like to be free, to have nothing more significant to think of than picking up his passport on the way out of the door.'

She looked down at Kizzy. 'Dan, I can't adopt her. I have to let her go. If I don't, I'll never be able to let go of Harry and move on.'

She was sleeping now, her little rosebud lips still white with milk, and carefully, so as not to wake her, Emily lifted her against her shoulder and walked with her until she brought up her wind, then carried her upstairs and changed her and put her down.

Then she went into Freddie's room and stared down at him, her baby, flat out on his back, arms and legs outstretched, sprawled the full length of his cot. He was outgrowing it, she realised. He'd need a bed soon. Maybe Beth's.

She was getting big for her little bed, but it would be perfect for Freddie.

And then who would have the cot?

No! She mustn't let herself think about it. It was madness. Anyway, he probably wouldn't want her to have Kizzy, because it would mean he would never be able to let her go, either. He'd always be thinking about her, and if he ever came back, he'd want to see her, and they'd never be able to move on, any of them.

And she wasn't foolish enough to imagine that one short hour in his arms would make any difference to him, no matter how wonderful it was. For her, at least.

For him, it had probably been simply a matter of propinquity. She'd been there, he'd felt a need to hold someone close.

Freddie stirred, his eyes flickered open and he smiled. 'Mummy,' he said, holding out his arms, and she lifted him from his cot and cradled him tight and inhaled the warm baby smell of him.

She'd been happy before Harry had come

back into her life—happy with Beth and Freddie and holding the fort for her parents, happy working for Nick and Georgie and doing other contracts locally.

Worried about money, yes, but happy, for all that. Contented. At peace.

Not so now. Now she was in turmoil, and she couldn't imagine it feeling any better for a long, long while.

If ever.

Georgie's baby was gorgeous.

Georgie was in the family room, ensconced on the sofa with the baby in her arms, and Harry and Dickon were playing with Maya on the floor.

'Oh, she's beautiful,' Emily breathed, her eyes filling as she set Kizzy's carrier down and hugged Georgie gently.

'She's really pretty,' Beth sighed, standing up on tiptoe and leaning over to get a better look.

'You think? I reckon she's got her father's nose.'

'There's nothing wrong with her father's nose,' Nick said, following them into the room with a grin he couldn't hide and an indulgent look about his eyes.

Emily reckoned if he could have crowed, he'd be doing it, and she laughed at him softly. 'I don't need to ask how the proud father's feeling this morning.'

He chuckled and sat down on the end of the sofa, scooping up Freddie and holding him so he could have a look. 'How about I take this lot out into the garden for a few minutes, give you two time to chat?'

Georgie smiled gratefully at him, and Nick ushered the children out through the French doors and into the garden, still within sight but out of earshot. Emily turned to her and took her friend's hand. 'So how are you? Really?'

'Really? Sore, a little bit battered and absolutely ecstatic. It's just wonderful. So different. Last year when we suddenly ended up with Harry and Dickon and Maya as a newborn baby, it was such a sad time. It shouldn't have been, Lucie dying was all wrong, and it was a time of massive adjustment for all of us. But this—this is just how it ought to be, another baby coming into the family, and oddly it doesn't feel all that different. I love the other three so much I can't imagine I'll love this one any more, but there is a difference. Carrying her, giving birth to her—it just makes it so much easier to love her. You know, I grew to love Maya, just as you've grown to love Kizzy, but I loved baby Lucie before she was born. Does that make sense?'

'Absolutely.' Emily nodded, thinking of Kizzy and how quickly she'd fallen under her spell, despite her best attempts to stay detached.

'I don't suppose there's any progress with you and Harry, is there? I'd so love to see you two settled. You belong together—you always have.'

'I don't think so.' She gave a strangled little laugh. 'Actually, I've got something to tell you. You know Harry's gone? He's in Indonesia, reporting on an earthquake.'

'Really? Oh, Emily, I didn't know! I'm so sorry—I haven't noticed anything but the baby since I went into labour.'

'No, well, I wouldn't expect you to. But anyway, just before he went, he told me…' She broke off, took a breath and went on, 'He said he was thinking of putting Kizzy up for adoption.'

Georgie's expression was horrified. 'Oh, Em, no! Oh, poor little thing! How can he?'

She shrugged. 'Says he can't be a full-time father and carry on with his job. And I don't know what to do. Dan says I should adopt her myself, but—I'll never be free of him if I do that. And it's so much worse this time.'

She closed her eyes, letting her head fall forward so her hair shielded her face, but Georgie just reached out an arm and drew her down, holding her while she cried.

'I miss him,' she sobbed. 'It's so silly. But I've been really stupid and let myself fall for him all over again, and now he's on the other side of the world and I just have this really bad feeling—'

'Hush. You've had that really bad feeling every time you've seen him reporting from some hellhole or other. You need to get him out of your system—sleep with him. Maybe it'll reveal some truly awful habits.'

Emily straightened up and sniffed, rummaging for a tissue. 'Nice theory. Unfortunately he doesn't seem to have any truly awful habits, so it didn't work.'

Georgie's jaw dropped. 'Oh, my, you've done it. After all this time.'

She nodded. 'Stupid. Stupid, stupid, stupid, but I just couldn't let him go without knowing—just in case. And now…'

'Oh, Em. I'm so sorry.'

She sniffed again and tried for a smile. 'No, I'm sorry. I should be here celebrating the baby with you, and all I can do is pour out my troubles. I'm a dreadful friend.'

'Rubbish. You're wonderful. Want to hold her?'

'I'd love to,' she said, and took the baby into her arms. 'Gosh, she feels heavier than Kizzy!'

'She probably is. She's a real porker, and Kizzy was very tiny.'

She nodded. 'She was. She's catching up now, though. Actually, there's something else I should tell you—something else I've done which is incredibly stupid and just makes letting her go even harder. I've started breastfeeding her.' She swallowed and forced herself to meet Georgie's eyes, waiting for the revulsion, but there was only sympathy and compassion.

'Oh, Em,' she whispered. 'Oh, how can you let her go? Now, after that?'

'Wet nurses always did.'

'They were usually poor women doing it for money or members of the same family. But you've done it for love.'

She looked down at little Lucie, and sighed. 'Yes. Yes, I have, but I shouldn't have done. It was silly, but it turns out that formula upsets her, so I don't know what would have happened if I hadn't been around.' She brushed her finger over Lucie's tiny palm, and it was immediately enclosed in a tight grasp. 'Oh, she's beautiful. Really strong. I'm so happy for you. I think you've been fantastic, both of you, taking on the kids, and I'm so glad you've got your own baby now. It just ties all of you together.'

She sighed and handed her back. 'I have to go. I've got work to do, and—'

'Television news to watch?' Georgie said astutely, and she gave a sad little laugh.

'Maybe. You get some rest. She'll be crawling before you know where you are. Enjoy her while she's tiny, it's over so very fast.'

'I will. And ring me—any time you want to talk. Or come over. You know you're always welcome.'

Emily hadn't lied.

She did have lots to do, not least bringing order to Harry's garden. If she could get it into some sort of shape before he came back, then it would be one less thing for them to have to deal with.

She was convinced they had no future. Sleeping with him had been rash and stupid—

and she wouldn't have changed it for the world, but it hadn't been her cleverest move. And she was more than ever certain that when he came back, he'd put the house on the market, give Kizzy up for adoption and that would be the last she'd see of him. If the garden was done, he'd be gone all the sooner and she could get back to normal.

She scrubbed the silly, foolish tears from her eyes and marshalled the children. 'Who fancies a picnic in the garden?' she said brightly. They chorused, 'Yes!' at the tops of their voices.

'Right, in the kitchen, everybody. Let's make it now. Uncle Dan?'

Uncle Dan unfolded himself from his chair, grabbed Beth and tickled her in passing and presented himself in the kitchen. 'Give me a job,' he said, and she handed him a pile of bread and the butter.

'Just a scrape,' she reminded him. 'We're having sandwiches.' And she busied herself pulling out food from the fridge and the cupboards, and refused to allow herself to think about Harry or what he might be doing…

It was horrendous.

The heat, the flies, the stench of bodies trapped beneath the buildings. Harry scrambled over the rubble in his path and walked down a street he'd known for years—a street now unrecognisable. The buildings had crumbled, the shops and houses falling in on each other, and everywhere there were desperate people digging.

He paused beside a house and spoke to a young man who was digging in the rubble with his bare hands. They were running with blood, but he didn't seem to notice.

'My wife and child,' he told Harry, and the dust on his face was streaked with tears. 'Just a baby. Help me.'

Harry's knowledge of the language was patchy, but the man's simple plea was universal. He questioned him a little more, then turned back to the cameraman.

'This is Ismael. His wife Rom is inside, with their two-week old baby son. He's desperate, because he can hear them crying, but there aren't enough rescue workers to help him find them, and time's running out. They won't have any food or water, and the baby's cries are so weak now he can hardly hear him. He's found a hole, and he's trying to clear it to see if he can get inside. I'm going to help him.'

He turned back to the man, tapped him on the shoulder and took the rock from his hands, lobbing it behind him. Together they shifted a large slab of what had once been wall out of the way, and crouched down, peering in through the hole. Ismael called his wife, and they heard a whimper from deep inside the building.

Fresh tears spilled over the man's cheeks, and he set about the rubble with renewed energy. Finally they shifted the last big lump of concrete out of the way, and the man lay down and squirmed in, calling as he went. He had a torch, and he was shining it around, then there was a shout from inside and Harry lay flat and stared after him.

There, in the mass of rubble and wood and twisted metal that had been their house, he saw a hand, reaching out, and he saw the man take it, clasping it as if his life depended on it.

Or hers.

He turned back to the camera. 'He's reached her. Tim, get help. I'm going in.'

'You can't, Harry!' the cameraman said, but Harry ignored him. He had no choice. There was enough room in there for two of them, and if they shifted that pile of rubble, there was a good chance they could get her out, or get medical aid to her. He shrugged off his jacket, emptied his pockets and crawled inside.

'Ismael,' he said, touching the man's leg, and he turned his head. 'Let me help. We can get her out.'

He could hear the shouts outside, the chorus going up, 'Survivors!'

But at that moment, as they were so close to success, he felt the ground gather itself.

No. Not again. Not another one, he thought, and as the shaking started, he heard the woman scream.

CHAPTER TEN

'Em?'

There was something about Dan's voice that sent a chill right through her. He was watching the news—something she'd steadfastly refused to allow herself to do—and she left her desk and went through to the sitting room.

Dan was standing there in front of the television, and he took her hand. 'Em, it's Harry, they're filming this live. He's pulling some crazy stunt. He's gone inside this house to help the man find his wife and baby, and—

The picture shuddered, and the cameraman exclaimed in shock, but he kept filming, live, on the other side of the world, as a cloud of dust rose up and the building shifted and settled.

She stared at it, her mouth open, and her heart all but stopped.

No.

Please, God, no.

She sat down abruptly and watched the rescue workers desperately trying to clear the rubble. The cameraman who'd been filming at the time was being interviewed now, and he was clearly shocked.

'I told him not to go in, but he just went anyway. He's never listened to reason, I guess this is just another of those occasions. We all do it and we try not to think about the consequences, but you never think it's going to happen to you.'

He turned back, staring at the rubble. 'I'm sorry, I can't talk to you. I have to help.'

And he went over to the gang working on the house and joined in, while Emily sat in shocked silence, twisting her hands together and forgetting to breathe.

'Dan, he's going to die,' she whispered. 'He may already…'

She broke off, distraught, and grabbed the remote control from his hand, switching to the satellite news and selecting the newsflash. Then Nick rang. Dan answered the phone, and a few minutes later he arrived to collect Beth and Freddie and take them to play. He'd seen the news, and knew what it would have done to her.

'Hang in there,' he said to Emily, hugging her, but she was numb.

All she could think of was Harry, the body she'd held so lovingly, that had brought her such joy, crushed by the weight of the rubble. All the tenderness, the passion, that wicked sense of humour and enormous energy snuffed out like a candle.

Kizzy woke, and she sat there in front of the endless news and fed his daughter while the tears streamed unheeded down her cheeks and her eyes stared unblinkingly at the unfolding drama before her.

God, he hurt.

Everywhere.

There was something pressing on his back and shoulders so he could scarcely breathe, and just beyond him he could hear Ismael's wife weeping. Ismael was silent, and he hadn't heard the baby cry at all.

He could hear rescue workers, though, the shouted instructions, the sound of machinery. And then they called for silence, and he tried to yell, but his breathing was so restricted he couldn't do more than whisper.

He could knock, though. He managed to make his hand into a fist around a rock, and he smacked it as hard as he could against the slab above him.

'I can hear something,' someone shouted, and he recognised the voice of Tim Daly, the came-raman.

He banged again, and again, and then he heard the scrape of a shovel and the urgent voices.

Thank God. He closed his eyes and assessed the situation.

He was lying on his front, his head turned to one side and his left arm twisted up behind his head. He must have lifted it up to protect his head and neck, but it was stuck now, and he didn't want to think about the pain. But he couldn't move at all. He could feel everything—only too well—but apart from his right arm and a very small amount of movement in his left leg, he was trapped. And if they managed to free him, he might end up with crush syndrome, from all the muscle proteins pouring into his bloodstream when the circulation was restored. And then he'd go into multiple organ failure and die.

He felt panic begin to rise, and squeezed his eyes shut, concentrating on slowing his breathing and not wasting energy. He wasn't getting enough oxygen into his body to waste it on futile panic.

So he thought about Em, and the baby, and how he would have felt if it had been them in here and he'd been in Ismael's place.

What was it Dan had said about being between a rock and a hard place? He nearly laughed, but the laugh turned to a sob, and he forced himself to be calm. He focussed on

Emily's face, the tender smile as she reached up and touched his mouth when he'd made love to her, her fingers exploring him.

He should have stayed there with her. He should have told his boss to go to hell, and stayed there with her, with the woman he loved, and with the family that had become his own.

But then he wouldn't have been there to help Ismael.

And Ismael might have been outside still when the aftershock had hit, instead of inside, lying still and silent while his wife wept at his side.

Just like Carmen, dead and cold in the hospital chapel while her tiny motherless daughter had struggled for life in the special care baby unit. All because he'd interfered.

He felt bile in his throat, but he could hardly swallow, and it seared his parched throat. He ignored it. Precious little else he could do, and all he could think about was Kizzy and what would become of her if he died.

If only Emily wasn't so set on not having her.

They'd make such a wonderful family, but she'd made it quite clear that she didn't want any more to do with her than was absolutely essential. Take the breast pump, for example. He'd thought it was crazy right from the start, taking the milk out of Emily into the pump and then a bottle to give to her, when the sensible, best and most convenient thing would have been to feed her directly.

But she'd been adamant, and who was he to argue? Just a relic from her past come back to complicate her carefully ordered existence.

It hadn't done a lot for his, either. Well, a lot for his existence, but damn all for the careful order. Or was it careless disorder he meant? Being able to walk out of the door at a moment's notice with nothing more than a phone, his wallet and his keys. A far cry from leaving the house with a baby. You had to be seriously orderly to achieve that. It was like a military operation.

He thought of his flat in London. He'd given Dan the keys the day before he'd left, so he could go and stay there. Was he still there? He hoped not, because when—if—he got out of this mess, he'd have to move back there.

Back there, alone, without Kizzy, without Em, without Beth and Freddie, without Nick and Georgie and their children. He wondered if they'd had the baby yet. Maybe not. It wasn't quite due, he didn't think, but he couldn't remember.

It seemed suddenly very important that he did, but he was losing focus. His right leg had gone to sleep, and his left arm was beginning to break through the mental block he'd put on it and give him hell. If only he could breathe…

It took ten hours to get him out.

Ten hours, during which Emily sat glued to the screen, watching the endless loop of tape until she knew it by heart, waiting for any further news to dribble through.

And then suddenly, without warning, they cut live to the scene where they'd been working all night, and they showed the rescue workers freeing him, lifting him carefully onto a sheet of corrugated iron and carrying him out.

Alive!

He was alive! His hand was moving, his legs shifting, and they cut to his face, battered and dusty, his mouth crusted and bleeding, and the emotion she'd held back for so many hours poured out in a torrent.

'Shh, baby, I've got you,' Dan said, cradling her against his chest, and she sobbed and sobbed, her eyes never leaving the screen as they carried him over the rubble and off down the street, Tim Daly, the cameraman, at his side.

'He'll be all right, won't he?' she asked, and Dan hesitated for a second and then nodded.

'Hopefully. At least he's alive. That's a good start.'

She straightened up and shot him a keen look. 'You think he could die? You do, don't you? Dan, he can't die. I can't live without him.'

She phoned the television centre but she got nowhere. She didn't know the name of his boss, and even if she had, who was she? A neighbour. That was all she could say. Not his lover, the woman looking after his baby. Not to the person on the switchboard. He might not want it to be common knowledge.

But she was desperate to get a message to him.

'Send him a text,' Dan said, reading her mind. 'He might have his phone on him.'

But it was lying in the rubble where he'd left it, together with the rest of the contents of his pockets, and it had been crushed beyond repair.

He was alive.

Sore—he gave a humourless laugh at that—but alive. His left arm was broken in two places and they'd pulled it out straight and put a cast on it without anaesthetic because he had been in danger of losing his hand because of the kinked arteries. That had been a bundle of laughs. And as for the rest of him, he was scraped and filthy and bruised to the point of Technicolor, but he was alive.

And so, to his relief, were Ismael and his wife and child. Ismael had a broken leg and concussion, but Rom and the baby were miraculously unharmed by their ordeal.

He went and saw them before he left the field hospital, and Rom took his bandaged hand and pressed it to her cheek and cried.

He hugged her gently, touched the baby's tiny hand with his bandaged finger and left them to it. They were all alive, and together. That was all that mattered. They were the lucky ones.

And so was he.

He knew what he had to do. Right now, before he did anything else.

But there was no reply, either on her house phone or her mobile, and he didn't feel he could leave a message. He didn't know what to say, in any case. He just knew he had to talk to her.

Face to face.

Yes. That was better. He'd do that.

Tim got him back to their base, helped him pack up his few things and took him to the airport.

'Good luck.'

'Thanks.'

Tim went to shake his hand, took one look at the bandages and hugged him instead. 'It's been good working with you, you crazy bastard,' he said, his voice choked, and then he let him go and gave him a little shove towards the departure lounge.

He needed no further encouragement.

There was no word from him.

She'd thought, in all the time that had elapsed, that either he or one of the team could have given her a call, but no. There had been nothing.

She knew he was all right. She'd seen him landing at Heathrow two hours ago, battered and bruised, his left eye swollen shut, his arm in a sling and both hands bandaged to the fingertips, but she'd had no word.

Well, what had she expected? That was Harry all over, dropping in and out of her life as if nothing had ever happened, breezing through and leaving her a mangled wreck in his wake.

She stared at the ceiling, wondering when he'd turn up. He would, of course. There was no question about that. He'd come back to sort out Kizzy, as he'd put it. And if she was stupid enough to encourage him, he'd probably stay for a while, but he'd go in the end, like he always had.

Well, she wouldn't encourage him. She'd let him make his arrangements for the baby, and she'd wave him goodbye and get on with her life.

Somehow.

She turned over and banged the pillow, but she couldn't sleep. She heard a car stop on the street, then drive on, and then a few moments later there was the sound of stones against her bedroom window.

What on earth…?

She heard it again, and got out of bed and peered round the curtain.

'Harry? What on earth are you doing?' she whispered hoarsly, throwing up the window and telling her heart to stop it, but he just grinned, and her heart flipped again and raced.

So did she, all the way downstairs, out of the back door and round the corner, straight into his arms. Well, arm. The other one was a hard line across her chest, and she realised it was in a cast.

'Ouch,' he said, laughing, and then the laughter died and his face contorted a little. His bandaged right hand came up to touch her face. 'It's nice to see you,' he said, and she gave a little hiccup of laughter that could just as easily have been a sob, and nodded.

'It's nice to see you, too. I wondered—when they showed it…'

She broke off, unable to finish, and he hugged her hard against his side with his right arm and led her into the house.

'Do you want a drink?' she asked, but he shook his head.

'All I want is to talk to you. To hold you. To try and let myself believe that I'm really here with you. But first I need to get my head down.'

'Do you want your keys?'

'Keys?'

'To your house. So you can go to bed.'

His eyes searched her face. 'Where's Dan?'

'Here. Upstairs in bed.'

'Then come with me.'

She shook her head. 'I'll need to feed Kizzy.'

'Can't Dan do it?'

She shook her head. 'No, because…' She looked away. 'I gave up with the pump. It seemed pointless. Wrong. So I need to be here. But you could stay,' she added, and then held her breath.

'Em?'

She shrugged. 'I know I shouldn't. I know you said you were going to give her up for adoption, and it'll tear me apart to let her go, but—it was all I could do for her, and you weren't here for her, and I just…'

'Oh, Em,' he breathed, and wrapped his arm around her. 'Come to bed with me. We need to talk, but I have to lie down. We'll go in your room.'

So they went upstairs, Harry limping slightly, his right leg reluctant to bend, and she led him into her bedroom, closed the door and undressed him, her eyes filling at the sight of the bruises.

'Sorry. It's a bit gaudy,' he said with a strained smile as she helped him ease back onto the mattress.

'You could have stuck to one part of the spectrum, instead of going for the whole rainbow,' she said, but her voice cracked unconvincingly and he sighed and drew her down against his chest.

'Come and lie next to me,' he murmured, and she lay down carefully and cuddled up, her head on his shoulder, worried about the bruises.

'Doesn't that hurt?' she asked, but he shook his head.

'Not so much that I'm going to let you go.' He turned his head and kissed her, just a brush of his poor, bruised lips against her brow, and she lifted her head and touched her mouth to his.

'Oh, Em,' he sighed, and his arm eased her closer. 'I thought I'd never see you again. I lay there, listening to Rom crying in the darkness, and I wondered if any of us would get out of there alive.'

'Rom?'

'Ismael's wife. She'd got a two-week-old baby in there with her. Em, if you'd seen the look on that man's face—heard his voice…'

'I did,' she told him. 'Tim was filming it. He filmed it all, right up to the aftershock, and then he put the camera down and left it running while he got help and joined in. Someone else picked it up and carried on filming, and they interviewed him, but he wouldn't talk, he wanted to help. They showed it live. I was watching when it all went shaky and the buildings shuddered, and I knew you were in there…'

She couldn't go on, couldn't relive it, and his arm tightened. 'Shh, it's OK, I'm here,' he said, and his mouth found hers again, his kiss urgent in the darkness.

He rolled towards her, his cast bumping against her hip, and she lifted her hand and cradled his jaw. 'Harry, we can't. It'll hurt you.'

'You'll have to be gentle, then, won't you?' he replied, and drew her tighter against his body. 'Because I need you, Em. Don't imagine for a moment that once was ever going to be enough.'

She took a ragged breath and let it out. 'I thought…it was goodbye.'

'No way. There's something you have to know. I've handed in my notice. You were right. It isn't what I am, it's just what I do. What I did. But there are other things, more important now. Other people can do my job. It's time for a change. In all sorts of ways.'

He shifted, his bandaged right hand stroking up and down her back, the touch strangely soothing. 'About Kizzy,' he said softly. 'How would you feel about adopting her?'

For a moment she thought she hadn't heard him right, because until that moment it had sounded as if there was hope for them, but this…?

'You ought to know, though,' he went on, his hand still stroking her, 'that she comes complete with her father. So if you did feel you wanted to take her on, you'd be taking me on, too. For better, for worse etcetera. And if you agreed, I'd very much like to adopt Beth and Freddie, too. So we all belonged to each other. Because I've realised that home isn't a place, it's the people, and my home is with you. You and Kizzy and Beth and Freddie. And I want to come home for good, Em. To you.'

He was holding his breath, she realised. His chest had frozen under her cheek, his heart thudding wildly.

'Oh, Harry,' she whispered, unable to speak. Instead she lifted her face to his, and kissed him.

'Well?' he demanded, his voice shaking, and she gave a funny little laugh that cracked in the middle.

'Oh, yes,' she said unsteadily. 'Yes, please. I can't think of anything I'd like more.'

His mouth found hers, cutting her off, and she lifted herself up so she could kiss him back better. Then gently, tenderly, so as not to hurt him, she eased out of his arms and settled down beside him.

'Hey!'

'Shh,' she told him. 'Just rest now. There's no hurry. We've got the rest of our lives ahead of us.'

And snuggling against his side, her hand over his, she listened as his breathing eased into sleep. He gave a soft snore, and her mouth kicked up into a contented smile.

So he did have some habits she'd have to get used to, she thought, but she didn't care. She'd embrace every one with joy.

Harry was finally home.

MILLS & BOON PUBLISH EIGHT LARGE PRINT TITLES A MONTH. THESE ARE THE EIGHT TITLES FOR MARCH 2008.

―――――❧―――――

THE BILLIONAIRE'S CAPTIVE BRIDE
Emma Darcy

BEDDED, OR WEDDED?
Julia James

THE BOSS'S CHRISTMAS BABY
Trish Morey

THE GREEK TYCOON'S UNWILLING WIFE
Kate Walker

WINTER ROSES
Diana Palmer

THE COWBOY'S CHRISTMAS PROPOSAL
Judy Christenberry

APPOINTMENT AT THE ALTAR
Jessica Hart

CARING FOR HIS BABY
Caroline Anderson

MILLS & BOON

Pure reading pleasure